A Bayard From Bengal by F. Anstey

F. Anstey was the pseudonym of Thomas Anstey Guthrie who was born in Kensington, London on August 8th, 1856, to Augusta Amherst Austen, an organist and composer, and Thomas Anstey Guthrie., a prosperous military tailor

Anstey was educated at King's College School and then at Trinity Hall, Cambridge. Although his education was first rate Anstey could only manage a third-class degree; A Gentlemen's degree as it was euphemistically known.

In 1880 he was called to the bar. However this career path rapidly fell away in his desire to become an author. The successful publication of Vice Versa, in 1882, with the premise of a substitution of a father for his schoolboy son, made his name and reputation as a refreshing and original humorist.

The following year he published a rather more serious work, The Giant's Robe. Interestingly the story is about a plagiarist and Anstey was, ironically, accused of plagiarism in writing the work. Despite good reviews both he and his public knew that his writing career was to be that of a humorist.

In the following years he published prolifically beginning with; The Black Poodle (1884), The Tinted Venus (1885), A Fallen Idol (1886), and Baboo Jabberjee B.A. (1897).

Anstey worked not only as a novelist and short story writer but was also a valued member of the staff at the humorous Punch magazine, in which his voces populi and his parodies of a reciter's stock-piece (Burglar Bill) represent perhaps his best work.

In 1901, his successful farce, The Man from Blankleys, based on a story that originally appeared in Punch, was first produced on stage at the Prince of Wales Theatre, in London.

Anstey had become a writer, and a successful one at that, of many talents.

Many more of his stories were made into plays and films over the years. Others were simply taken for the premise alone, usually with no credit to the original author.

By the end of the First World War Anstey's original publications had slowed to a crawl and he seemed rather more interested in translating and publishing some works of Moliere.

Thomas Anstey Guthrie died of pneumonia on March 10th, 1934 in London.

His self-deprecating autobiography, A Long Retrospect, was published in 1936.

Index of Contents

PRELIMINARY
CHAPTER I - FROM CALCUTTA TO CAMBRIDGE OVERSEA ROUTE
CHAPTER II - HOW MR BHOSH DELIVERED A DAMSEL FROM A DEMENTED COW
CHAPTER III - THE INVOLUNTARY FASCINATOR

CHAPTER IV - A KICK FROM A FRIENDLY FOOT
CHAPTER V - THE DUEL TO THE DEATH
CHAPTER VI - LORD JOLLY IS SATISFIED
CHAPTER VII - THE ADVENTURE OF THE UNWIELDY GIFTHORSE
CHAPTER VIII - A RIGHTABOUT FACER FOR MR BHOSH
CHAPTER IX - THE DARK HORSE
CHAPTER X - TRUST HER NOT! SHE IS FOOLING THEE!
CHAPTER XI - STONE WALLS DO NOT MAKE A CAGE
CHAPTER XII - A RACE AGAINST TIME
CHAPTER XIII - A SENSATIONAL DERBY STRUGGLE
CHAPTER XIV - A GRAND FINISH
THE PARABLES OF PILJOSH
F. ANSTEY – A CONCISE BIBLIOGRAPHY

PRELIMINARY

I have the honour humbly to inform my readers that, after prolonged consumption of midnight oil, I succeeded in completing this imposing society novel, which is now, by the indulgence of my friends and kind fathers, the honble publishers, laid at their feet.

My inducement to this enterprise was the spectacle of very inferior rubbish palmed off by so-called popular novelists such as Honbles Kipling, Joshua Barrie, Antony Weyman, Stanley Hope, and the collaborative but feminine authoresses of "The Red Thumb in the Pottage," all of whom profess (very, very incorrectly) to give accurate reliable descriptions of Indian, English or Scotch episodes.

The pity of it, that a magnificent and gullible British Public should be suckled like a babe on such spoonmeat and small beer!

Would no one arise, inflamed by the pure enthusiasm of his cacoethes scribendi, and write a romance which shall secure the plerophory of British, American, Anglo-Indian, Colonial, and Continental readers by dint of its imaginary power and slavish fidelity to Nature?

And since Echo answered that no one replied to this invitation, I (like a fool, as some will say) rushed in where angels were apprehensive of being too bulky to be borne.

Being naturally acquainted with gentlemen of my own nationality and education, and also, of course, knowing London and suburban society ab ovo usque ad mala (or, from the new-laid egg to the stage when it is beginning to go bad), I decided to take as my theme the adventures of a typically splendid representative of Young India on British soil, and I am in earnest hopes to avoid the shocking solecisms and exaggerations indulged in by ordinary English novelists.

I have been compelled to take to penmanship of this sort owing to pressure of res angusta domi, the immoderate increase of hostages to fortune, and proportionate falling off of emoluments from my profession as Barrister-at-Law.

Therefore, I hope that all concerned will smile favourably upon my new departure, and will please kindly understand that, if my English literary style has suffered any deterioration, it is solely due to my being out of practice, and such spots on the sun must be excused as mere flies in ointment.

After forming my resolution of writing a large novel, I confided it to my crony, Mr Ram Ashootosh Lall, who warmly recommended me to persevere in such a magnum opus. So I became divinely inflated periodically every evening from 8 to 12 P.M., disregarding all entreaties from feminine relatives to stop and indulge in a blow-out on ordinary eatables, like Archimedes when Troy was captured, who was so engrossed in writing prepositions on the sand that he was totally unaware that he was being barbarously slaughtered.

And at length my colossal effusion was completed, and I had written myself out; after which I had the indescribable joy and felicity to read my composition to my mothers-in-law and wives and their respective progenies and offspring, whereupon, although they were not acquainted with a word of English, they were overcome by such severe admiration for my fecundity and native eloquence that they swooned with rapture.

I am not superstitious, but I took the trouble to consult a soothsayer, as to the probable fortunes of my undertaking, and he at once confidently predicted that my novel was to render all readers dumb as fishes with sheer amazement and prove a very fine feather in my cap.

For all the above reasons, I am modestly confident that it will be generally recognised as a masterpiece, especially when it is remembered that it is the work of a native Indian, whose 'prentice hand is still a novice in wielding the currente calamo of fiction.

I cannot conclude without some allusion to the drawings which are, I believe, to adorn my work, but which I have not yet been enabled to inspect, owing to the fact that, having fish of more importance to fry at the time, I commissioned a certain young English friend (the same who furnished sundry poetic headings for chapters) to engage a designer for the pictorial department.

Needless to say, I intended that he was to award the apple only to some Royal Academician of distinguished talents—yet at the eleventh hour, when too late to make other arrangements, I am informed that the job has been entrusted to a certain Birnadhur Pahtridhji, whose name (though probably incorrectly transcribed) certainly denotes a draughtsman of native Indian origin!

Whether he is fully competent for such a task I cannot at present say. But, unless he is qualified, like myself, by actual residence in Great Britain, I fear that he may not possess sufficient familiarity with the customs and solecisms of English society to avoid at least a few ludicrous and even lamentable mistakes.

To guard against such contingencies I shall insert a note or comment opposite each picture as it is submitted to me, pointing out in what respects (if any) the artist has failed to represent the author's intentions.

I sincerely hope that I may now and then be able to pat the aforesaid Mr P. on the back instead of acting as a Rhadamanthus to rap his knuckles.

CHAPTER I

FROM CALCUTTA TO CAMBRIDGE OVERSEA ROUTE

At sea the stoutest stomach jerks, Far, far away from native soil, When Ocean's heaving waterworks Burst out in Brobdingnagian boil!

The waves of Neptune erected their seething and angry crests to incredible altitudes; overhead in fuliginous storm-clouds the thunder rumbled its terrific bellows, and from time to time the ghastly flare of lightning illuminated the entire neighbourhood. The tempest howled like a lost dog through the cordage of the good ship Rohilkund (Captain O. Williams), which lurched through the vasty deep as though overtaken by the drop too much.

At one moment her poop was pointed towards celestial regions; at another it aimed itself at the recesses of Davey Jones's locker; and such was the fury of the gale that only a paucity of the ship's passengers remained perpendicular, and Mr Chunder Dindabun Dhosh was recumbent on his beam end, prostrated by severe sickishness, and hourly expecting to become initiated in the Great Secret.

Bitterly did he lament his hard lines in venturing upon the Black Water, to be snipped off in the flower of his adolescence, and never again to behold the beloved visages of his relations!

So heartrending were his tears and groans that they moved all on board, and Honble Mr Commissioner Copsey, who was returning on leave, kindly came to inquire the cause of such vociferous lachrymation.

"What is the matter, Baboo?" began the Commissioner in paternal tones. "Why are you kicking up the shindy of such a deuce's own hullabaloo?"

"Because, honble Sir," responded Mr Bhosh, "I am in lively expectation that waters will rush in and extinguish my vital spark."

"Pooh!" said Mr Commissioner, genially. "This is only the moiety of a gale, and there is not the slightest danger."

Having received this assurance, Mr Bhosh's natural courage revived, and, coming up on deck, he braved the tempest with the cool composure of a cucumber, admonishing all his fellow-passengers that they were not to give way to panic, seeing that Death was the common lot of all, and, though everyone must die once, it was an experience that could not be repeated, with much philosophy of a similar kind which astonished many who had falsely supposed him to be a pusillanimous.

The remainder of the voyage was uneventful, and, soon after setting his feet on British territory, Mr Bhosh became an alumnus and undergraduate of the Alma Mater of Cambridge.

I shall not attempt to relate at any great length the history of his collegiate career, because, being myself a graduate of Calcutta University, I am not, of course, proficient in the customs and etiquettes of any rival seminaries, and should probably make one or two trivial slips which would instantly be pounced upon and held up for derision by carping critics.

So I shall content myself with mentioning a few leading facts and incidents. Mr Bhosh very soon wormed himself into the good graces of his fellow college boys, and his principal friend and fidus Achates was a young high-spirited aristocrat entitled Lord Jack Jolly, the only son of an earl who had lately been promoted to the dignity of a baronetcy.

Lord Jolly and Mr Bhosh were soon as inseparable as a Dæmon and Pythoness, and, though no nabob to wallow in filthy lucre, Mr Bhosh gave frequent entertainments to his friends, who were hugely delighted by the elegance of his hospitality and the garrulity of his conversation.

Unfortunately the fame of these Barmecide feasts soon penetrated the ears of the College gurus, and Mr Bhosh's Moolovee sent for him and severely reprimanded him for neglecting to study for his Little-go degree, and squandering his immense abilities and talents on mere guzzling.

Whereupon Mr Bhosh shed tears of contrition, embracing the feet of his senile tutor, and promising that, if only he was restored to favour he would become more diligent in future.

And honourably did he fulfil this nudum pactum, for he became a most exemplary bookworm, burning his midnight candle at both ends in the endeavour to cram his mind with belles lettres.

But he was assailed by a temptation which I cannot forbear to chronicle. One evening as he was poring over his learned tomes, who should arrive but a deputation of prominent Cambridge boatmen and athletics, to entreat him to accept a stroke oar of the University eight in the forthcoming race with Oxford College!

This, as all aquatics will agree, was no small compliment—particularly to one who was so totally unversed in wielding the flashing oar. But the authorities had beheld him propelling a punt boat with marvellous dexterity by dint of a paddle, and, taking the length of his foot on that occasion, they had divined a Hercules and ardently desired him as a confederate.

Mr Bhosh was profoundly moved: "College misters and friends," he said, "I welcome this invitation with a joyful and thankful heart, as an honour—not to this poor self, but to Young India. Nevertheless, I am compelled by Dira Necessitas to return the polite negative. Gladly I would help you to inflict crushing defeat upon our presumptuous foe, but 'I see a hand you cannot see that beckons me away; I hear a voice you cannot hear that wheezes "Not to-day!"' In other words, gentlemen, I am now actively engaged in the Titanic struggle to floor Little-go. It is glorious to obtain a victory over Oxonian rivals, but, misters, there is an enemy it is still more glorious to pulverize, and that enemy is—one's self!"

The deputation then withdrew with falling crests, though unable to refrain from admiring the firmness and fortitude which a mere Native student had nilled an invitation which to most European youths would have proved an irresistible attraction.

Nor did they cherish any resentment against Mr Bhosh, even when, in the famous inter-collegiate race of that year from Hammersmith to Putney, Cambridge was ingloriously bumped, and Oxford won in a common canter.

CHAPTER II

Mr Bhosh's diligence at his books was rewarded by getting through his Little-go with such éclat that he was admitted to become a baccalaureate, and further presented with the greatest distinction the Vice-Chancellor could bestow upon him, viz., the title of a Wooden Spoon!

But here I must not omit to narrate a somewhat startling catastrophe in which Mr Bhosh figured as the god out of machinery. It was on an afternoon before he went up to pass his Little-go exam, and, since all work and no play is apt to render any Jack a dull, he was recreating himself by a solitary promenade in some fields in the vicinity of Cambridge, when suddenly his startled ears were dumbfounded to perceive the blood-curdling sound of loud female vociferations!

On looking up from his reverie, he was horrified by the spectacle of a young and beauteous maiden being vehemently pursued by an irate cow, whose reasoning faculties were too obviously, in the words of Ophelia, "like sweet bells bangled," or, in other words, non compos mentis, and having rats in her upper story!

The young lady, possessing the start and also the advantage of superior juvenility, had the precedence of the cow by several yards, and attained the umbrageous shelter of a tree stem, behind which she tremulously awaited the arrival of her blood-thirsty antagonist.

As he noted her jewel-like eyes, profuse hair, and panting bosom, Mr Bhosh's triangle of flesh[1] was instantaneously ignited by love at first sight (the intelligent reader will please understand that the foregoing refers to the maiden and not at all to the cow, which was of no excessive pulchritude—but I am not to be responsible for the ambiguities of the English language).

[1] Videlicet: his heart.

There was not a moment to be squandered; Mr Bhosh had just time to recommend her earnestly to remain in statu quo, before setting off to run ventre à terre in the direction whence he had come. The distracted animal, abandoning the female in distress, immediately commenced to hue-and-cry after our hero, who was compelled to cast behind him his collegiate cap, like tub to a whale.

The savage cow ruthlessly impaled the cap on one of its horns, and then resumed the chase.

Mr Bhosh scampered for his full value, but, with all his incredible activity, he had the misery of feeling his alternate heels scorched by the fiery snorts of the maniacal quadruped.

Then he stripped from his shoulders his student's robe, relinquishing it to the tender mercies of his ruthless persecutress while he nimbly surmounted a gate. The cow only delayed sufficiently to rend the garment into innumerable fragments, after which it cleared the gate with a single hop, and renewed the chase after Mr Bhosh's stern, till he was forced to discard his ivory-headed umbrella to the animal's destroying fury.

This enabled him to gain the walls of the town and reach the bazaar, where the whole population was in consternation at witnessing such a shuddering race for life, and made themselves conspicuous by their absence in back streets.

Mr Bhosh, however, ran on undauntedly, until, perceiving that the delirious creature was irrevocably bent on running him to earth, he took the flying leap into the shop of a cheese merchant, where he cleverly entrenched himself behind the receipt of custom.

With the headlong impetuosity of a distraught the cow followed, and charged the barrier with such insensate fury that her horns and appertaining head were inextricably imbedded in a large tub of margarine butter.

At this our hero, judging that the wings of his formidable foe were at last clipped, sallied boldly forth, and, summoning a police-officer, gave the animal into custody as a disturber of the peace.

By such coolness and savoir faire in a distressing emergency he acquired great kudos in the eyes of all his fellow-students, who regarded him as the conquering hero.

Alas and alack! when he repaired to the field to receive the thanks and praises of the maiden he had so fortunately delivered, he had the mortification to discover that she had vanished, and left not a wreck behind her! Nor with all his endeavours could he so much as learn her name, condition, or whereabouts, but the remembrance of her manifold charms rendered him moonstruck with the tender passion, and notwithstanding his success in flooring the most difficult exams, his bosom's lord sat tightly on its throne, and was not to jump until he should again (if ever) confront his mysterious fascinator.

Having emerged from the shell of his statu pupillari under the fostering warmth of his Alma Mater, Mr Bhosh next proceeded as a full-fledged B.A. to the Metropolis, and became a candidate for forensic honours at one of the legal temples, lodging under the elegant roof of a matron who regarded him as her beloved son for Rs. 21 per week, and attending lectures with such assiduity that he soon acquired a nodding acquaintance with every branch of jurisprudence.

And when he went up for Bar Exam., he displayed his phenomenal proficiency to such an extent that the Lord Chancellor begged him to accept one of the best seats on the Judges' bench, an honour which, to the best of this deponent's knowledge and belief, has seldom before been offered to a raw tyro, and never, certainly, to a young Indian student. However, with rare modesty Mr Bhosh declined the offer, not considering himself sufficiently ripe as yet to lay down laws, and also desirous of gathering roses while he might, and mixing himself in first-class English societies.

I am painfully aware that such incidents as the above will seem very mediocre and humdrum to most readers, but I shall request them to remember that no hero can achieve anything very striking while he is still a hobbardehoy, and that I cannot—like some popular novelists—insult their intelligences by concocting cock-and-bull occurrences which the smallest exercise of ordinary commonsense must show to be totally incredible.

By and bye, when I come to deal with Mr Bhosh's experiences in the upper tenth of London society, with which I may claim to have rather a profound familiarity, I will boldly undertake that there shall be no lack of excitement.

Therefore, have a little patience, indulgent Misters!

CHAPTER III

THE INVOLUNTARY FASCINATOR

Mr Bhosh was very soon enabled to make his debût as a pleader, for the Mooktears sent him briefs as thick as an Autumn leaf in Vallambrosa, and, having on one occasion to prosecute a youth who had embezzled an elderly matron, Mr Bhosh's eloquence and pathos melted the jury into a flood of tears which procured the triumphant acquittal of the prisoner.

But the bow of Achilles (which, as Poet Homer informs us, was his only vulnerable point) must be untied occasionally, and accordingly Mr Bhosh occasionally figured as the gay dog in upper-class societies, and was not long in winning a reputation in smart circles as a champion bounder.

For he did greet those he met with a pleasant, obsequious affability and familiarity, which easily endeared him to all hearts. In his appearance he would—but for a somewhat mediocre stature and tendency to a precocious obesity—have strikingly resembled the well-known statuary of the Apollo Bellevue, and he was in consequence inordinately admired by aristocratic feminines, who were enthralled by the fluency of his small talk, and competed desperately for the honour of his company at their "Afternoon-At-Home-Teas."

It was at one of these exclusive festivities that he first met the Duchess Dickinson, and (as we shall see hereafter) that meeting took place in an evil-ominous hour for our hero. As it happened, the honourable highborn hostess proposed a certain cardgame known as "Penny Napkin," and fate decreed that Mr Bhosh should sit contiguous to the Duchess's Grace, who by lucky speculations was the winner of incalculable riches.

But, hoity toity! what were his dismay and horror, when he detected that by her legerdemain in double-dealing she habitually contrived to assign herself five pictured cards of leading importance!

How to act in such an unprecedented dilemma? As a chivalrous, it was repugnant to him to accuse a Duchess of sharping at cards, and yet at the same time he could not stake his fortune against such a foregone conclusion!

So he very tactfully contrived by engaging the Duchess's attention to substitute his card-hand for hers, and thus effect the exchange which is no robbery, and she, finally observing his finesse, and struck by the delicacy with which he had so unostentatiously rebuked her duplicity, earnestly desired his further acquaintance.

For a time Mr Bhosh, doubtless obeying one of those supernatural and presentimental monitions which were undreamt of in the Horatian philosophy, resisted all her advances—but alas! the hour arrived in which he became as Simpson with Delilah.

It was at the very summit of the Season, during a brilliantly fashionable ball at the Ladbroke Hall, Archer Street, Bayswater, whither all the élites of tip-top London Society had congregated.

Mr Bhosh was present, but standing apart, overcome with bashfulness at the paucity of upper feminine apparel and designing to take his premature hook, when the beauteous Duchess in passing surreptitiously flung over him a dainty nose-handkerchief deliciously perfumed with extract of cherry blossoms.

With native penetration into feminine coquetries he interpreted this as an intimation that she desired to dance with him, and, though not proficient in such exercises, he made one or two revolutions round the room with her co-operation, after which they retired to an alcove and ate raspberry ices and drank lemonade. Mr Bhosh's sparkling tittle-tattle completely achieved the Duchess's conquest, for he possessed that magical gift of the gab which inspired the tender passion without any connivance on his own part.

And, although the Duchess was no longer the chicken, having attained her thirtieth lustre, she was splendidly well preserved; with huge flashing eyes like searchlights in a face resembling the full moon; of tall stature and proportionate plumpness; most young men would have been puffed out by pride at obtaining such a tip-top admirer.

Not so our hero, whose manly heart was totally monopolised by the image of the fair unknown whom he had rescued at Cambridge from the savage clutches of a horned cow, and although, after receiving from the Duchess a musk-scented postal card, requesting his company on a certain evening, he decided to keep the appointed tryst, it was only against his will and after heaving many sighs.

On reaching the Duchess's palace, which was situated in Pembridge Square, Bayswater, he had the mortification to perceive that he was by no means the only guest, since the reception halls were thickly populated by gilded worldlings. But the Duchess advanced to greet him in a very kind, effusive manner, and, intimating that it was impossible to converse with comfort in such a crowd, she led him to a small side-room, where she seated him on a couch by her side and invited him to discourse.

Mr Bhosh discoursed accordingly, paying her several high-flown compliments by which she appeared immoderately pleased, and discoursed in her turn of instinctive sympathies, until our hero was wriggling like an eel with embarrassment at what she was to say next, and at this point Duke Dickinson suddenly entered and reminded his spouse in rather abrupt fashion that she was neglecting her remaining guests.

After the Duchess's departure, Mr Bhosh, with the feelings of an innate gentleman, felt constrained to make his sincere apologies to his ducal entertainer for having so engrossed his better half, frankly explaining that she had exhibited such a marked preference for his society that he had been deprived of all option in the matter, further assuring his dukeship that he by no means reciprocated the lady's sentiments, and delicately recommending that he was to keep a rather more lynxlike eye in future upon her proceedings.

To which the Duke, greatly agitated, replied that he was unspeakably obliged for the caution, and requested Mr Bhosh to depart at once and remain an absentee for the future. Which our friend cheerfully undertook to perform, and, in taking leave of the Duchess, exhorted her, with an eloquence that moved all present, to abandon her frivolities and levities and adopt a deportment more becoming to her matronly exterior.

The reader would naturally imagine that she would have been grateful for so friendly and well-meant a hint—but oh, dear! it was quite the reverse, for from a loving friend she was transformed into a bitter and most unscrupulous enemy, as we shall find in forthcoming chapters.

Truly it is not possible to fathom the perversities of the feminine disposition!

CHAPTER IV

A KICK FROM A FRIENDLY FOOT

Mr Bhosh's bosom-friend, the Lord Jack Jolly, had kindly undertaken to officiate as his Palinurus and steer him safely from the Scylla to the Charybdis of the London Season, and one day Lord Jolly arrived at our hero's apartments as the bearer of an invite from his honble parent the Baronet, to partake of tiffin at their ancestral abode in Chepstow Villas, which Bindabun gratefully accepted.

Arrived at the Jollies' sumptuous interior, a numerous retinue of pampered menials and gilded flunkies divested Mr Bhosh of his hat and umbrella and ushered him into the hall of audience.

"Bhosh, my dear old pal," said Lord Jack, "I have news for you. I am engaged as a Benedict, and am shortly to celebrate matrimony with a young good-looking female—the Princess Petunia Jones."

"My lord," replied Mr Bhosh, "suffer me to hang around your patrician neck the floral garland of my humble congratulations."

"My dear Bhosh," responded the youthful peer of the realm, "I regard you as more than a brother, and am confident that when my betrothed beholds your countenance, she will conceive for you a similar lively affection. But hush! here she comes to answer for herself.... Princess, permit me to present to you the best and finest friend I possess, Mr Bindabun Bhosh."

Mr Bhosh modestly lowered his optics as he salaamed with inimitable grace, and it was not until he had resumed his perpendicular that he recognised in the Princess Jones the charming unknown whom he had last beheld engaged in repelling the assault of a distracted cow!

Their eyes were no sooner crossed than he knew that she regarded him as her deliverer, and was consumed by the most ardent affection for him. But Mr Bhosh repressed himself with heroic magnanimity, for he reflected that she was the affianced of his dearest friend and that it was contrary to bon ton to poach another's jam.

So he merely said; "How do you do? It is a very fine day. I am delighted to make your acquaintance," and turning on his heels with a profound curtsey, he left her flabbergasted with mortification.

But those only who have compressed their souls in the shoe of self-sacrifice know how devilishly it pinches, and Mr Bhosh's grief was so acute that he rolled incessantly on his couch while the radiant image of his divinity danced tantalisingly before his bloodshot vision.

Eventually he became calmer, and after plunging his fervid body into a foot-bath, he showed himself once more in society, assuming an air of meretricious waggishness to conceal the worm that was busily cankering his internals, and so successful was he that Lord Jack was entirely deceived by his vis comica, and invited him to spend the Autumn up the country with his respectable parents.

Mr Bhosh accepted—but when he knew that Princess Petunia was also to be one of the amis de la maison, he was greatly concerned at the prospect of infallibly reviving her love by his propinquity, and thereby inflicting the cup of calamity on his best friend. Willingly would he have imparted the whole truth to his Lordship and counselled him to postpone the Princess's visit until he, himself, should have departed—but, ah me! with all his virtue he was not a Roman Palladium that he should resist the delight of philandery with the radiant queen of his soul. So he kept his tongue in his cheek.

However, when they met in the ancient and rural castle he constrained himself, in conversing with her, to enlarge enthusiastically upon the excellences of Lord Jack. "What a good, ripping, gentlemanly fellow he was, and how certain to make a best quality husband!" Princess Jones listened to these encomiums with tender sighing, while her soft large orbs rested on Mr Bhosh with ever-increasing admiration.

No one noticed how, after these elephantine efforts at self-denial, he would silently slip away and weep salt and bitter tears as he weltered dolefully on a doormat; nor was it perceived that the Princess herself was become thin as a weasel with disappointed love.

Being the ardent sportsman, Mr Bhosh sought to drown his sorrow with pleasures of the chase.

He would sally forth alone, with no other armament than a breech-loading rifle, and endeavour to slay the wild rabbits which infested the Baronet's domains, and sometimes he had the good fortune to slaughter one or two. Or he would take a Rod and hooks and a few worms, and angle for salmons; or else he would stalk partridges, and once he even assisted in a foxhunt, when he easily outstripped all the dogs and singly confronted Master Reynard, who had turned to bay savagely at his nose. But Bindabun undauntedly descended from his horse, and, drawing his hunting dagger, so dismayed the beast by his determined and ferocious aspect that it turned its tail and fled into some other part of the country, which earned him the heartfelt thanks from his fellow Nimrods.

Naturally, such feats of arms as these only served to inflame the ardour of the Princess, to whom it was a constant wonderment that Mr Bhosh did never, even in the most roundabout style, allude to the fact that he had saved her life from perishing miserably on the pointed horn of an enraged cow.

She could not understand that the Native temperament is too sheepishly modest to flaunt its deeds of heroism.

Those who are au fait in knowledge of the world are aware that when there are combustibles concealed in any domestic interior, there is always a person sooner or later who will contrive to blow them off; and here, too, the Serpent of Mischief was waiting to step in with cloven hoof and play the very deuce.

It so happened that the Duchess occupied the adjacent bungalow to that of Baronet Jolly and his lady, with whom she was hail-fellow-well-met, and this perfidious female set herself to ensnare the confidence of the young and innocent Princess by discreetly lauding the praises of Mr Bhosh.

"What an admirable Indian Crichton! How many rabbits and salmons had he laid low that week? Truly, she regarded him as a favourite son, and marvelled that any youthful feminine could prefer an ordinary peer like Lord Jolly to a Native paragon who was not only a university B.A., but had successfully passed Bar Exam!" and so forth and so on.

The princess readily fell into this insidious booby-trap, and confessed the violence of her attachment, and how she had striven to acquaint Mr Bhosh with her sentiments but was rendered inarticulate by maidenly bashfulness.

"Can you not then slip a love-letter into his hand?" inquired the Duchess.

"Cui bono?" responded the Princess, sadly. "Seeing that he never approaches near enough to me to receive such a missive, and I dare not entrust it to one of my maidens!"

"Why not to Me?" said the Duchess. "He will not refuse it coming from myself; moreover, I have influence over him and will soften his heart towards thee."

Accordingly the Princess indicted a rather impassioned love-letter, in which she assured Mr Bhosh that she had divined his secret passion and fully reciprocated it, also that she was the total indifferent to Lord Jack, with much other similar matters.

Having obtained possession of this litera scripta, what does the unscrupulous Duchess next but deliver it impromptu into the hands of Lord Jack, who, after perusing it, was overcome by uncontrollable wrath and instantaneously summoned our hero to his presence.

Here was the pretty kettle of fish—but I must reserve the sequel for the next chapter.

CHAPTER V

THE DUEL TO THE DEATH

No sooner had Mr Bhosh obeyed the summons of Lord Jack, than the latter not only violently reproached him for having embezzled the heart of his chosen bride, but inflicted upon him sundry severe kicks from behind, barbarously threatening to encore the proceeding unless Chunder instantaneously agreed to meet him in a mortal combat.

Our hero, though grievously hurt, did not abandon his presence of mind in his tight fix. Seating himself upon a divan, so as to obviate any repetition of such treatment, he thus addressed his former friend: "My dear Jack, Plato observes that anger is an abbreviated form of insanity. Do not let us fall out about so mere a trifle, since one friend is the equivalent of many females. Is it my fault that feminines overwhelm me with unsought affections? Let us both remember that we are men of the world, and if you on your side will overlook the fact that I have unwittingly fascinated your fiancée, I, on mine, am ready to forget my unmerciful kickings."

But Lord Jolly violently rejected such a give-and-take compromise, and again declared that if Mr Bhosh declined to fight he was to receive further kicks. Upon this Chunder demanded time for reflection; he was no bellicose, but he reasoned thus with his soul: "It is not certain that a bullet will hit—whereas, it is impossible for a kick to miss its mark."

So, weeping to find himself between a deep sea and the devil of a kicking, he accepted the challenge, feeling like Imperial Cæsar, when he found himself compelled to climb up a rubicon after having burnt his boots!

Being naturally reluctant to kick his brimming bucket of life while still a lusty juvenile, Mr Bhosh was occupied in lamenting the injudiciousness of Providence when he was most unexpectedly relieved by the entrance of his lady-love, the Princess Jones, who, having heard that her letter had fallen into Lord Jack's hands, and that a sanguinary encounter would shortly transpire, had cast off every rag of maidenly propriety, and sought a clandestine interview.

She brought Bindabun the gratifying intelligence that she was a persona grata with his lordship's seconder, Mr Bodgers, who was to load the deadly weapons, and who, at her request, had promised to do so with cartridges from which the bullets had previously been bereft.

Such a piece of good news so enlivened Mr Bhosh, that he immediately recovered his usual serenity, and astounded all by his perfect nonchalance. It was arranged that the tragical affair should come off in the back garden of Baronet Jolly's castle, immediately after breakfast, in the presence of a few select friends and neighbours, among whom—needless to say—was Princess Petunia, whose lamp-like optics beamed encouragement to her Indian champion, and the Duchess of Dickinson, who was now the freehold tenement of those fiendish Siamese twins—Malice and Jealousy. At breakfast, Mr Bhosh partook freely of all the dishes, and rallied his antagonist for declining another fowl-egg, rather wittily suggesting that he was becoming a chicken-hearted. The company then adjourned to the garden, and all who were non-combatants took up positions as far outside the zone of fire as possible.

Mr Bhosh was rejoiced to receive from the above-mentioned Mr Bodgers a secret intimation that it was the put-up job, and little piece of allright, which emboldened him to make the rather spirited proposal to his lordship, that they were to fire—not at the distance of one hundred paces, as originally suggested —but across the more restricted space of a nosekerchief. This dare-devilish proposal occasioned a universal outcry of horror and admiration; Mr Bhosh's seconder, a young poor-hearted chap, entreated him to renounce his plan of campaign, while Lord Jack and Mr Bodgers protested that it was downright tomfolly.

Chunder, however, remained game to his backbone. "If," he ironically said, "my honble friend prefers to admit that he is inferior in physical courage to a native Indian who is commonly accredited with a funky heart, let him apologise. Otherwise, as a challenged, I am the Master of the Ceremonies. I do not insist upon the exchange of more than one shoot—but it is the sine quâ non that such shoot is to take place across a nosewipe."

Upon which his lordship became green as grass with apprehensiveness, being unaware that the cartridges had been carefully sterilised, but glueing his courage to the sticky point, he said, "Be it so, you blood-thirsty little beggar—and may your gore be on your own knob!"

"It is always barely possible," retorted Mr Bhosh, "that we may both miss the target!" And he made a secret motion to Mr Bodgers with his superior eyeshutter, intimating that he was to remember to omit the bullets.

But lackadaisy! as Poet Burns sings, the best-laid schemes both of men and in the mouse department are liable to gang aft—and so it was in the present instance, for Duchess Dickinson intercepted Chunder

Bindabun's wink and, with the diabolical intuition of a feminine, divined the presence of a rather suspicious rat. Accordingly, on the diaphanous pretext that Mr Bodgers was looking faintish and callow, she insisted on applying a very large smelling-jar to his nasal organ.

Whether the vessel was charged with salts of superhuman potency, or some narcotic drug, I am not to inquire—but the result was that, after a period of prolonged sternutation, Mr Bodgers became impercipient on a bed of geraniums.

Thereupon Chunder, perceiving that he had lost his friend in court, magnanimously said: "I cannot fight an antagonist who is unprovided with a seconder, and will wait until Mr Bodgers is recuperated." But the honourable and diabolical duchess nipped this arrangement in the bud. "It would be a pity," said she, "that Mr Bhosh's fiery ardour should be cooled by delay. I am capable to load a firearm, and will act as Lord Jolly's seconder."

Our hero took the objection that, as a feminine was not legally qualified to act as seconder in mortal combats, the duel would be rendered null and void, and appealed to his own seconder to confirm this obiter dictum.

Unluckily the latter was a poor beetlehead who was in excessive fear of offending the Duchess, and gave it as his opinion that sex was no disqualification, and that the Duchess of Dickinson was fully competent to load the lethal weapons, provided that she knew how.

Whereupon she, regarding Mr Bhosh with the malignant simper of a fiend, did not only deliberately fill each pistol-barrel with a bullet from her own reticule bag, but also had the additional diablerie to extract a miniature laced mouchoir exquisitely perfumed with cherry-blossoms, and to say, "Please fire across this. I am confident that it will bring you good luck."

And Mr Bhosh recognised with emotions that baffle description the very counterpart of the nose-handkerchief which she had flung at him months previously at the aforesaid fashionable Bayswater Ball! Now was our poor miserable hero indeed up the tree of embarrassment—and there I must leave him till the next chapter.

CHAPTER VI

LORD JOLLY IS SATISFIED

Many a more hackneyed duellist than our unfortunate friend Bhosh might well have been frightened from his propriety at the prospect of fighting with genuine bullets across so undersized a nosekerchief as that which the Duchess had furnished for the fray.

But Mr Bhosh preserved his head in perfect coolness: "It is indisputably true," he said, "that I proposed to shoot across a pocketkerchief—but I am not an effeminate female that I should employ such a lacelike and flimsy concern as this! As a challenged, I claim my constitutional right under Magna Charta to provide my own nosewipe."

And, as even my Lord Jack admitted that this was legally correct, Mr Bhosh produced a very large handsome nosekerchief in parti-coloured silks.

This he tore into narrow strips, the ends of which he tied together in such a manner that the whole was elongated to an incredible length. Then, tossing one extremity to his lordship, and retaining the other in his own hand, he said: "We will fight, if you please, across this—or not at all!"

Which caused a working majority of the company, and even Lord Jack Jolly himself, to burst into enthusiastic plaudits of the ingenuity and dexterity with which Mr Bhosh had contrived to extricate himself from the prongs of his Caudine fork.

The Duchess, however, was knitting her brows into the baleful pattern of a scowl—for she knew as well as Chunder Bindabun himself that no human pistol was capable to achieve such a distance! The duel commenced. His lordship and Mr Bhosh each removed their upper clothings, bared their arms, and, taking up a weapon, awaited the momentous command to fire.

It was pronounced, and Lord Jolly's pistol was the first to ring the ambient welkin with its horrid bang. The deadly missile, whistling as it went for want of thought, entered the door of a neighbouring pigeon's house and fluttered the dovecot confoundedly.

Mr Bhosh reserved his fire for the duration of two or three harrowing seconds. Then he, too, pulled off his trigger, and after the explosion there was a loud cry of dismay.

The bullet had perforated a large circular orifice in Honble Bodger's hat, who, by this time, had returned to self-consciousness!

"I could not bring myself to snuff the candle of your honble lordship's existence," said Mr Bhosh, bowing, "but I wished to convince all present that I am not incompetent to hit a mark."

And he proceeded to assure Mr Bodger that he was to receive full compensation for any moral and intellectual damage done to his said hat.

As for his lordship, he was so overcome by Mr Bhosh's unprecedented magnanimity that he shed copious tears, and, warmly embracing his former friend, entreated his forgiveness, vowing that in future their affection should never again be endangered by so paltry and trivial a cause as the ficklety of a feminine. Moreover, he bestowed upon Bindabun the blushing hand of Princess Jones, and very heartily wished him joy of her.

Now the Princess was the solitary brat of a very wealthy merchant prince, Honble Sir Monarch Jones, whose proud and palatial storehouses were situated in the most fashionable part of Camden Town.

Sir Jones, in spite of Lord Jack's resignation, did not at first regard Mr Bhosh with the paternal eye of approval, but rather advanced the objection that the colour of his money was practically invisible. "My daughter," he said haughtily, "is to have a lakh of rupees on her nuptials. Have you a lakh of rupees?"

Bindabun was tempted to make the rather facetious reply that he had, indeed, a lack of rupees at the present moment.

Sir Monarch, however, like too many English gentlemen, was totally incapable of comprehending the simplest Indian jeu des mots, and merely replied. "Unless you can show me your lakh of rupees, you cannot become my beloved son-in-law."

So, as Mr Bhosh was a confirmed impecunious, he departed in severe despondency. However, fortune favoured him, as always, for he made the acquaintance of a certain Jewish-Scotch, whose cognomen was Alexander Wallace McAlpine, and who kindly undertook to lend him a lakh of rupees for two days at interest which was the mere bite of a flea.

Having thus acquired the root of all evil, Bindabun took it in a four-wheeled cab and triumphantly exhibited his hard cash to Sir Jones, who, being unaware that it was borrowed plumage, readily consented that he should marry his daughter. After which Mr Bhosh honourably restored the lakh to the accommodating Scotch minus the interest, which he found it inconvenient to pay just then.

I am under great apprehensions that my gentle readers, on reading thus far and no further, will remark: "Oho! then we are already at the finis, seeing that when a hero and heroine are once booked for connubial bliss, their further proceedings are of very mediocre interest!"

Let me venture upon the respectful caution that every cup possesses a proverbially slippery lip, and that they are by no means to take it as granted that Mr Bhosh is so soon married and done for.

Remember that he still possesses a rather formidable enemy in Duchess Dickinson, who is irrevocably determined to insert a spike in his wheel of fortune. For a woman is so constituted that she can never forgive an individual who has once treated her advances with contempt, no matter how good-humoured such contempt may have been. No, misters, if you offend a feminine you must look out for her squalls.

Readers are humbly requested not to toss this fine story aside under the impression that they have exhausted the cream in its cocoanut. There are many many incidents to come of highly startling and sensational character.

CHAPTER VII

THE ADVENTURE OF THE UNWIELDY GIFTHORSE

In accordance with English usages, Mr Bhosh, being now officially engaged to the fair Princess Jones, did dance daily attendance in her company, and, she being passionately fond of equitation, he was compelled himself to become the Centaur and act as her cavalier servant on a nag which was furnished throughout by a West End livery jobber. Fortunately, he displayed such marvellous dexterity and skill as an equestrian that he did not once sustain a single reverse!

Truly, it was a glorious and noble sight to behold Bindabun clinging with imperturbable calmness to the saddle of his steed, as it ambled and gamboled in so spirited a manner that all the fashionables made sure that he was inevitably to slide over its tail quarters! But invariably he returned, having suffered no further inconvenience than the bereavement of his tall hat, and the heart of Princess Petunia was uplifted with pride when she saw that her betrothed, in addition to being a B.A. and barrister-at-law, was also such a rough rider.

It is de rigueur in all civilised societies to encourage matrimony by bestowing rewards upon those who are about to come up to the scratch of such holy estate, and consequently splendid gifts of carriage, timepieces, tea-caddies, slices of fish, jewels, blotter-cases, biscuit-caskets, cigar-lights, and pin-cushions were poured forth upon Mr Bhosh and his partner, as if from the inexhaustibly bountiful horn of a Pharmacopoeia.

Last, but not least, one morning appeared a saice leading an unwieldy steed of the complexion of a chestnut, and bearing an anonymously-signed paper, stating that said horse was a connubial gift to Mr Bhosh from a perfervid admirer.

Our friend Bindabun was like to throw his bonnet over the mills with excessive joy, and could not be persuaded to rest until he had made a trial trip on his gifted horse, while the amiable Princess readily consented to become his companion.

So, on a balmy and luscious afternoon in Spring, when the mellifluous blackbirds, sparrows, and other fowls of that ilk were engaged in billing and cooing on the foliage of innumerable trees and bushes, and the blooming flowers were blowing proudly on their polychromatic beds, Mr Bhosh made the ascension of his gifthorse, and titupped by the side of his betrothed into the Row, the observed of all the observing masculine and feminine smarties.

But, hoity-toity! he had not titupped very many yards when the unwieldy steed came prematurely to a halt and adopted an unruly deportment. Mr Bhosh inflicted corporal punishment upon its loins with a golden-headed whip, at which the rebellious beast erected itself upon its hinder legs until it was practically a biped.

Bindabun, although at the extremity of his wits to preserve his saddle by his firm hold on the bridle-rein, undauntedly aimed a swishing blow at the head and front of the offending animal, which instantaneously returned its forelegs to terra firma, but elevated its latter end to such a degree that our hero very narrowly escaped sliding over its neck by cleverly clutching the saddleback.

Next, the cantankerous steed executed a leap with astounding agility, arching its back like a bow, and propelling our poor friend into the air like the arrow, though by providential luck and management on his part he descended safely into his seat after every repetition of this dangerous manoeuvre.

All things, however, must come to an end at some time, and the unwieldy quadruped at last became weary of leaping and, securing the complete control of his bit, did a bolt from the blue.

Willy nilly was Mr Bhosh compelled to accompany it upon its mad, unbridled career, while all witnesses freely hazarded the conjecture that his abduction would be rather speedily terminated by his being left behind, and I will presume to maintain that a less practical horseman would long before have become an ordinary pedestrian.

But Bindabun, although both stirrupholes were untenanted, and he was compelled to hold on to his steed's mane by his teeth and nails, nevertheless remained triumphantly in the ascendant.

On, on he rushed, making the entire circumference of the Park in his wild, delirious canter, and when the galloping horse once more reappeared, and Mr Bhosh was perceived to be still snug on his saddle, the spectators were unable to refrain from heartfelt joy.

A second time the incorrigible courser careered round the Park on his thundering great hoofs, and still our heroic friend preserved his equilibrium—but, heigh-ho! I have to sorrowfully relate that, on his third circuit, it was the different pair of shoes—for the headstrong animal, abstaining from motion in a rather too abrupt manner, propelled Mr Bhosh over its head with excessive velocity into the elegant interior of a victoria-carriage.

He alighted upon a great dame who had maliciously been enjoying the spectacle of his predicament, but who now was forced to experience the crushing repartee of his tu quoque, for such a forcible collision with his person caused her not only two blackened optics but irremediable damage to the leather of her nose.

The pristine beauty of her features was irrecoverably dismantled, while Mr Bhosh—thanks to his landing on such soft and yielding material—remained intact and able to return to his domicile in a four-wheeled cab.

Beloved reader, however sceptical thou mayest be, thou wilt infallibly admire with me the inscrutable workings of Nemesis, when thou learnest that the aforesaid great lady was no other than the Duchess of Dickinson, and (what is still more wonderful) that it was she who had insidiously presented him with such a fearful gift of the Danaides as an obstreperous and unwieldy steed!

Truly, as poet Shakespeare sagaciously observes, there is a divinity that rough-hews our ends, however we may endeavour to preserve their shapeliness!

CHAPTER VIII

A RIGHTABOUT FACER FOR MR BHOSH

Those who are au faits in the tortoise involutions of the feminine disposition will hear without astonishment that Duchess Dickinson—so far from being chastened and softened by the circumstance that the curse she had launched at Mr Bhosh's head had returned, like an illominous raven, to roost upon her own nose and irreparably destroy its contour—was only the more bitterly incensed against him.

Instead of interring the hatchet that had flown back, as if it were that fabulous volatile the boomerang, she was in a greater stew than ever, and resolved to leave no stone unturned to trip him up. But what trick to play, seeing that all the honours were in Mr Bhosh's hands?

She could not officiate as Marplot to discredit him in the affections of his lady-love, since the Princess was too severely enamoured to give the loan of her ear to any sibillations from a snake in grass.

How else, then, to hinder his match? At this she was seized with an idea worthy of Maccaroni himself. She paid a complimentary visit to the Princess, arrayed in the sheepish garb of a friend, and contrived to lure the conversation on to the vexed question of prying into futurity.

Surely, she artfully suggested, the Princess at such a momentous epoch of her existence had, of course, not neglected the sensible precaution of consulting some competent soothsayer respecting the most propitious day for her nuptials with the accomplished Mr Bhosh?...

What, had she omitted to pop so important a question? How incredibly harebrained! Fortunately, there was yet time to do the needful, and she herself would gladly volunteer to accompany the Princess on such an errand.

Princess Petunia fell a ready victim into the jaws of this diabolical booby-trap and inquired the address and name of the cleverest necromancer, for it is matter of notoriety that London ladies are quite as superstitious and addicted to working the oracle as their native Indian sisters.

The Duchess replied that the Astrologer-Royal was a facile princeps at uttering a prediction, and accordingly on the very next day she and the Princess, after disguising themselves, set forth on the summit of a tramway 'bus to the Observatory Temple of Greenwich, where, after first propitiating the prophet by offerings, they were ushered into a darkened inner chamber. Although they were strictly pseudo, he at once informed them of their genuine cognomens, and also told them much concerning their past of which they had hitherto been ignorant.

And to the Princess he said, stroking the long and silvery hairs of his beard, "My daughter, I foresee many calamities which will inevitably befall thee shouldest thou marry before the day on which the bridegroom wins a certain contest called the Derby with a horse of his own."

The gentle Petunia departed melancholy as a gib cat, since Mr Bhosh was not the happy possessor of so much as a single racing-horse of any description, and it was therefore not feasible that he should become entitled to wear the cordon bleu of the turf in his buttonhole on his wedding day!

With many sighs and tears she imparted her piece of news to the horror-stricken ears of our hero, who earnestly assured her that it was contrary to commonsense and bonos mores, to attach any importance to the mere ipse dixit of so antiquated a charlatan as the Astrologer-Royal, who was utterly incapable—except at very long intervals—to bring about even such a simple affair as an eclipse which was visible from his own Observatory!

However, the Princess, being a feminine, was naturally more prone to puerile credulities, and very solemnly declared that nothing would induce her to kneel by Mr Bhosh's side at the torch of Hymen until he should first have distinguished himself as a Derby winner.

Whereat Mr Bhosh, perceiving that the date of his nuptial ceremony was become a dies non in a Grecian calendar, did wring his hands in a bath of tears.

Alas! he was totally unaware that it was his implacable enemy, the Duchess Dickinson, who had thus upset his apple-cart of felicity—but so it was, for by a clandestine bribe, she had corrupted the Astrologer-Royal—a poor, weak, very avaricious old chap—to trump out such a disastrous prediction.

Some heroes in this hard plight would have thrown up the leek, but Mr Bhosh was stuffed with sterner materials. He swore a very long oath by all the gods that he had ceased to believe in, that sooner or later, by crook or hook, he would win the Derby race, though entirely destitute of horseflesh and very ill able to afford to purchase the most mediocre quadruped.

Here some sporting readers will probably object! Why could he not enlist his unwieldy gifthorse among Derby candidates and so hoist the Duchess on the pinnacle of her own petard?

To which I reply: Too clever by halves, Misters! Imprimis, the steed in question was of far too ferocious a temperament (though undeniably swift-footed) ever to become a favourite with Derby judges; secondly, after dismounting Mr Bhosh, it had again taken to its heels and departed into the Unknown, nor had Mr Bhosh troubled himself to ascertain its private address.

But fortune favours the brave. It happened that Mr Bhosh was one day promenading down the Bayswater Road when he was passed by a white horse drawing a milk chariot with unparalleled velocity, outstripping omnibuses, waggons, and even butcher carts in its wind-like progress, which was unguided by any restraining hand, for the milk-charioteer himself was pursuing on foot.

His natural puissance in equine affairs enabled Mr Bhosh to infer that the steed which could cut such a record when handicapped with a cumbrous dairy chariot would exhibit even greater speed if in puris naturalibus, and that it might even not improbably carry off first prize in the Derby race.

So, as the milk-charioteer ran up, overblown with anxiety, to learn the result of his horse's escapade, Mr Bhosh stopped him to inquire what he would take for such an animal.

The dairy-vendor, rather foolishly taking it for granted that horse and cart were gone concerns, thought he was making the good stroke of business in offering the lot for a twenty-pound note.

"I have done with you!" cried Mr Bhosh sharply, handing over the purchase-money, which he very fortunately chanced to have about him, and galloping off to inspect his bargain, which was like buying a pig after once poking it in the ribs.

In what condition he found it I must leave you to learn, my dear readers, in an ensuing chapter.

CHAPTER IX

THE DARK HORSE

It is a gain, a precious, let me gain! let me gain! Oh, Potentate! Oh, Potentate! The shower of thine secret shoe-dust Oh, Potentate! Oh, Potentate!

We left Mr Bhosh in full pursuit of the runaway horse and milk-chariot which he had so spiritedly purchased while still en route. After running a mile or two, he was unspeakably rejoiced to find that the equipage had automatically come to a standstill and was still in prime condition—with the exception of the lacteal fluid, which had made its escape from the pails.

Bindabun, however, was not disposed to weep for long over spilt milk, and had the excessive magnanimity to restore the chariot and pails to the dairy merchant, who was beside himself with gratitude.

Then, Mr Bhosh, with a joyful heart, having detached his purchase from the shafts, conducted it in triumph to his domicile. It turned out to be a mare, white as snow and of marvellous amiability; and, partly because of her origin, and partly from her complexion, he christened her by the appellation of Milky Way.

Although perforce a complete ignoramus in the art of educating a horse to win any equine contest, Mr Bhosh's nude commonsense told him that the first step was to fatten his rather too filamentous pupil with corn and similar seeds, and after a prolonged course of beanfeasts he had the gratification to behold his mare filling out as plump as a dumpling.

As he desired her to remain the dark horse as long as possible, he concealed her in a small toolshed at the end of the garden, ministering to her wants with his own hands, and conducting her for daily nocturnal constitutionals several times round the central grass-patch.

For some time he refrained from mounting—"fain would he climb but that he feared to fall," as Poet Bunyan once scratched with a diamond on Queen Anne's window; but at length, reflecting that if nothing ventures nothing is certain to win, he purchased a padded saddle with appendages, and surmounted Milky Way, who, far from regarding him as an interloper, appeared gratified by his arrival, and did her utmost to make him feel thoroughly at home.

The next step was, of course, to obtain permission from the pundits who rule the roast of the Jockey Club, that Milky Way might be allowed to compete in the approaching Derby.

Now this was a more delicately ticklish matter than might be supposed, owing to the circumstance that the said pundits are such warm men, and so well endowed with this world's riches that they are practically non-corruptible.

Fortunately, Mr Bhosh, as a dabster in English composition, was a pastmaster in drawing a petition, and, sitting down, he constructed the following:—

TO THOSE MOST WORSHIPFUL BIGHEADS IN CONTROL OF JOCKEYS CLUB.

BENIGN PERSONAGES!

This Petition humbly sheweth:

(1.) That your Petitioner is a native Indian Cambridge B.A., a Barrister-at-law, and a most loyal and devoted subject of Her Majesty the QUEEN-EMPRESS.

(2.) That it is of excessive importance to him, for private reasons, that he should win a Derby Race.

(3.) That such a famous victory would be eminently popular with all classes of Indian natives, and inordinately increase their affection for British rule.

(4.) That for some time past your Petitioner has been diligently training a quadruped which he fondly hopes may gain a victory.

(5.) That said quadruped is a member of the fair sex.

(6.) That she is a female horse of very docile disposition, but, being only recently extracted from shafts of dairy chariot, is a total neophyte in Derby racing.

(7.) That your lordships may direct that she is to be kindly permitted to try her luck in this world-famous competition.

(8.) That it would greatly encourage her to exhibit topmost speed if she could be allowed to start running a few minutes previously to older stagers.

(9.) That if this is unfortunately contrary to regulations, then the Judge should receive secret instructions to look with a favourable eye upon the said female horse (whose name is Milky Way) and award her first prize, even if by any chance she may not prove quite so fast a runner as more professional hacks:

And your Petitioner will ever pray on bended knees that so truly magnificent an institution as the Epsom Derby Course may never be suppressed on grounds of encouraging national vice of gambling and so forth. Signed, &c.

The wording of the above proved Mr Bhosh's profound acquaintance with the human heart, for it instantaneously attained the desired end.

The Honble Stewards returned a very kind answer, readily consenting to receive Milky Way as a candidate for Derby honours, but regretting that it was ultra vires to concede her a few minutes' start, and intimating that she must start with a scratch in company with all the other horses.

Bindabun was not in the least degree cast down or depressed by this refusal of a start, since he had not entertained any sanguine hope that it would be granted, and had only inserted it to make insurance doubly sure, for he was every day more confident that Milky Way was to win, even though obliged to step off with the rank and file.

CHAPTER X

TRUST HER NOT! SHE IS FOOLING THEE!

Now that our hero had obtained that the name of Milky Way was to be inscribed on the Golden Book of Derby candidates, his next proceeding was to hire a practical jockey to assume supreme command of her.

And this was no simple matter, since practical jockeys are usually hired many weeks beforehand, and demand handsome wages for taking their seats. But at last, after protracted advertisements, Mr Bhosh had the good fortune to pitch upon a perfect treasure, whose name was Cadwallader Perkin, and who, for his riding in some race or other, had been awarded a whole year's holiday by the stewards who had observed the paramountcy of his horsemanship.

No sooner had Perkin inspected Milky Way than he was quite in love with his stable companion, and assured his employer that, with more regular out-of-door exercise, she would be easily competent to win the Derby on her head, whereupon Mr Bhosh consented that she should be galloped after dark round the inner circle of Regent's Park, which is chiefly populated at such a time by male and female bicyclists.

But in order to pay Perkins charges, and also provide a silken jockey tunic and cap of his own racing colours (which were cream and sky-blue), Mr Bhosh was compelled to borrow more money from Mr McAlpine, who, as a Jewish Scotch, exacted the rather exorbitant interest of sixty per centum.

It leaked out in some manner that Milky Way was a coming Derby favourite, and the property of a Native young Indian sportsman, whose entire fortunes depended on her success, and soon immense multitudes congregated in Regent's Park to witness her trials of speed, and cheered enthusiastically to behold the fiery sparks scintillating from the stones as she circumvented the inner circle in seven-leagued boots.

Mr Bhosh of course asseverated that she was a very mediocre sort of mare, and that he did not at all expect that she would prove a winner, but connoisseurs nevertheless betted long odds upon her success, and Bindabun himself, though not a speculative, did put on the pot himself upon the golden egg which he was so anxiously hatching.

One evening amongst those who were gathered to view the nocturnal exercises of Milky Way there appeared a feminine spectator of rather sinister aspect, in a thick veil and a victoria-carriage.

It was no other than Duchess Dickinson, who had somehow learnt how courageously Mr Bhosh was endeavouring to fulfil the Astrologer-Royal's prediction, and who had come to ascertain whether his mare was indeed such a paragon of celerity as had been represented.

The very first time that Milky Way cantered past with the gait of a streak of lightning, the Duchess realised with a sinking heart that Mr Bhosh must indubitably succeed at the Derby—unless he was prevented.

But how to achieve this? Her womanly instinct told her that Cadwallader Perkin was far too inexperienced to resist for long such mature and ripened charms as hers—even though the latter were unfortunately discounted by the accidental nose-flattening.

So, lowering her veil till only her eyes were visible above, she waited till he passed once more, then flung him such a liquid and flashing glance from her starry and now no longer discoloured optics that the young jockey, who was of an excessively susceptible disposition, all but fell off the saddle with emotion, like a very juvenile bird under serpentine observation.

"He is mine!" said the unscrupulous Duchess internally, laughing up her sleeve at such a proof of her fascinations, "mine! mine!"

She had too much intelligence and mother-wit, however, to take any steps until Mr Bhosh should be safely out of the way—and how to accomplish his removal?

As an acquaintance with the above-mentioned usurer, McAlpine, she was aware that he had advanced large loans to Mr Bhosh, and so she laid her plans and bided her time.

There soon remained only one day before that carnival of all sporting saturnalians, the Epsom Derby day, and Bindabun formed the prudent resolution to avoid any delays or crushings by putting Milky Way into a railway box, and despatching her to Epsom on the previous afternoon, under the chaperonage of Cadwallader Perkin, who was to engage suitable lodgings for her in the vicinity of the course.

But just as Bindabun was approaching the booking hole of Victoria terminus to take a horse-ticket, lo and behold! he was rapped on the shoulder by a couple of policemen, who civilly inquired whether his name was not Bhosh.

He replied that it was, and that he was the lucky proprietor of a female horse who was infallibly destined to win the Derby, and that he was even now proceeding to purchase her travelling ticket. But the policemen insisted that he must first discharge the full amount of his debt and costs to Mr McAlpine, who had commenced a law-suit.

"It is highly inconvenient to pay now," replied our hero, "I will settle up after receiving my Derby Stakes."

"We are infernally sorry," said the constables, "but we have instructions to imprison you until the amount is stumped up, and anything you say now will be taken down and used against you at your trial."

Mr Bhosh remained sotto voce; and as he was being led off with gyves upon his wrists, like Aram the usher, whom should he behold but the Duchess of Dickinson!

Like all truly first-class heroes, he was of a generous, confiding nature, and his head was not for a moment entered by the suspicion that the Duchess could still cherish any ill feelings towards him. "I am sincerely sorry," he said with good-humoured gallantry, "to observe that your ladyship's nose-leather is still in such bad repair. I was riding a rather muscular steed that afternoon, and could not thoroughly control my movements."

She suavely responded that she was proud to have been the means of breaking his fall.

"Not only my fall—but your own nose!" retorted Mr. Bhosh sympathetically. "A sad pity! Fortunately, at your time of life such disfigurements are of no consequence. I, myself, am now in the pretty pickle."

And he explained how he had been arrested for debt, at the very moment when he had an appointment to meet his mare and jockey and see them safely off by the Epsom train.

"Do not trouble about that," said the Duchess. "Hand me your purse, and I myself will meet them and do the needful on your behalf. I have interest with this Mr McAlpine and will intercede that you are let out immediately."

Mr Bhosh kissed her hand as he handed over his said purse. "This is, indeed, a noble return for my coldheartedness," he said, "and I am even more sorry than before that I should have involuntarily dilapidated so exquisite a nose."

"Pray do not mention it," replied the Duchess, with the baleful simper of a Sphynx, and Mr Bhosh departed for his durance vile with a mind totally free from misgivings.

CHAPTER XI

STONE WALLS DO NOT MAKE A CAGE

Oh, give me back my Arab steed, I cannot ride alone! Or tell me where my Beautiful, my four-legged bird has flown. 'Twas here she arched her glossy back, beside the fountain's brink, And after that I know no more—but I came off, I think.

More so-called original lines by aforesaid young English friend. But I have the shrewd suspicion of having read them before somewhere.—H. B. J.

And now, O gentle and sympathetic reader, behold our unfortunate hero confined in the darkest bowels of the Old Bailey Dungeon, for the mere crime of being an impecunious!

Yes, misters, in spite of all your boasted love of liberty and fresh air, imprisonment for debt is still part of the law of the land! How long will you deafen your ears to the pitiable cry of the bankrupt as he pleads for the order of his discharge? Perhaps it has been reserved for a native Indian novelist to jog the elbow of so-called British jurisprudence, and call its attention to such a shocking scandal.

Mr Bhosh found his prison most devilishly dull. Some prisoners have been known to beguile their captivity by making pets or playmates out of most unpromising materials. For instance, and exempli gratia, Mr Monty Christo met an abbey in his dungeon, who gave him a tip-top education; Mr Picciola watered a flower; the Prisoner of Chillon made chums of his chains; while Honble Bruce, as is well-known, succeeded in taming a spider to climb up a thread and fall down seven times in succession.

But Mr Bhosh had no spider to amuse him, and the only flowers growing in his dungeon were toadstools, which do not require to be watered, nor did there happen to be any abbey confined in the Old Bailey at the time.

Nevertheless, he was preserved from despair by his indomitable native chirpiness. For was not Milky Way a dead set for the Derby, and when she came out at the top of the pole, would he not be the gainer of sufficient untold gold to pay all his debts, besides winning the hand of Princess Petunia?

He was waited upon by the head gaoler's daughter, a damsel of considerable pulchritude by the name of Caroline, who at first regarded him askance as a malefactor.

But, on learning from her parent that his sole offence was insuperable pennilessness, her tender heart was softened with pity to behold such a young gentlemanly Indian captive clanking in bilboes, and soon they became thick as thieves.

Like all the inhabitants of Great Britain, her thoughts were entirely engrossed with the approaching Derby Race, and she very innocently narrated how it was matter of common knowledge that a notorious grandame, to wit the fashionable Duchess of Dickinson, had backed heavily that Milky Way was to fail like the flash of a pan.

Whereupon Mr Bhosh, recollecting that he had actually entrusted his invaluable mare with her concomitant jockey to the mercy of this self-same Duchess, was harrowed with sudden misgivings.

By shrewd cross-questions he soon eliminated that Mr McAlpine was a pal of the Duchess, which she had herself admitted at the Victoria terminus, and thus by dint of penetrating instinct, Mr Bhosh easily unravelled the tangled labyrinth of a hideous conspiracy, which caused him to beat his head vehemently against the walls of his cell at the thought of his utter impotentiality.

Like all feminines who were privileged to make his acquaintance, Miss Caroline was transfixed with passionate adoration for Bindabun, whom she regarded as a gallant and illused innocent, and resolved to assist him to cut his lucky.

To this end she furnished him with a file and a silken ladder of her own knitting—but unfortunately Mr Bhosh, having never before undergone incarceration, was a total neophyte in effecting his escape by such dangerous and antiquated procedures, which he firmly declined to employ, urging her to sneak the paternal keybunch and let him out at daybreak by some back entrance.

And, not to crack the wind of this poor story while rendering it as short as possible, she yielded to his entreaties and contrived to restore him to the priceless boon of liberty the next morning at about 5 A.M.

Oh, the unparalleled raptures of finding himself once more free as a bird!

It was the dawn of the Derby Day, and Mr Bhosh precipitated himself to his dwelling, intending to array himself in all his best and go down to Epsom, where he was in hopes of encountering his horse. Heyday! What was his chagrin to see his jockey, Cadwallader Perkin, approach with streaming eyes, fling himself at his master's feet and implore him to be merciful!

"How comes it, Cadwallader," sternly inquired Mr Bhosh, "that you are not on the heath of Epsom instead of wallowing like this on my shoes?"

"I do not know," was the whimpered response.

"Then pray where is my Derby favourite, Milky Way?" demanded Bindabun.

"I cannot tell," wailed out the lachrymose juvenile. Then, after prolonged pressure, he confessed that the Duchess had met him at the station portals, and, on the plea that there was abundance of spare time to book the mare, easily persuaded him to accompany her to the buffet of Refreshment-room.

There she plied him with a stimulant which jockeys are proverbially unable to resist, viz., brandy-cherries, in such profusion that he promptly became catalyptic in a corner.

When he returned to sobriety neither the Duchess nor the mare was perceptible to his naked eye, and he had been searching in vain for them ever since.

It was the time not for words, but deeds, and Mr Bhosh did not indulge in futile irascibility, but sat down and composed a reply wire to the Clerk of Course, Epsom, couched in these simple words: "Have you seen my Derby mare?—BHOSH."

After the suspense of an hour the reply came in the discouraging form of an abrupt negative, upon which Mr Bhosh thus addressed the abashed Perkin: "Even should I recapture my mare in time, you have proved yourself unworthy of riding her. Strip off your racing coat and cap, and I will engage some more reliable equestrian."

The lad handed over the toggery, which Bindabun stuffed, being of very fine silken tissue, into his coat pocket, after which he hurried off to Victoria in great agitation to make inquiries.

There the officials treated his modest requests in very off-handed style, and he was becoming all of a twitter with anxiety and humiliation, when, mirabile dictu! all of a sudden his ears were regaled by the well-known sound of a whinny, and he recognised the beloved voice of Milky Way!

But whence did it proceed? He ran to and fro in uncontrollable excitement, endeavouring to locate the sound. There was no trace of a horse in any of the waiting-rooms, but at length he discovered that his mare had been locked up in the Left-Luggage department, and, summoning a porter, Mr Bhosh had at last the indescribable felicity to embrace his kidnapped Derby favourite Milky Way!

CHAPTER XII

A RACE AGAINST TIME

There's a certain old Sprinter; you've got to be keen, If you'd beat him—although he is bald, And he carries a clock and a mowing-machine. On the cinderpath "Tempus" he's called.

Stanza written to order by young English friend, but (I fear) copied from Poet Tennyson.

Ah! with what perfervid affection did Mr Bhosh caress the neck of his precious horse! How carefully he searched her to make sure that she had sustained no internal poisonings or other dilapidations!

Thank goodness! He was unable to detect any flaw within or without—the probability being that the crafty Duchess did not dare to commit such a breach of decorum as to poison a Derby favourite, and thought to accomplish her fell design by leaving the mare as lost luggage and destroying the ticket-receipt.

But old Time had already lifted the glass to his lips, and the contents were rapidly running down, so Mr Bhosh, approaching a railway director, politely requested him to hook a horse-box on to the next Epsom train.

What was his surprise to hear that this could not be done until all Derby trains had first absented themselves! With passionate volubility he pleaded that, if such a law of Medes and Persians was to be insisted on, Milky Way would infallibly arrive at Epsom several hours too late to compete in the Derby race, in which she was already morally victorious—until at length the official relented, and agreed to do the job for valuable consideration in hard cash.

Lackadaisy! after excavating all his pockets, our unhappy hero could only fork out wherewithal enough for third-class single ticket for himself, and he accordingly petitioned that his mare might travel as baggage in the guard's van.

I am not to say whether the officials at this leading terminus were all in the pay of the Duchess, since I am naturally reluctant to advance so serious a charge against such industrious and talented parties, but it is nem. con. that Mr Bhosh's very reasonable request was nilled in highly offensive cut-and-dried fashion, and he was curtly recommended to walk himself and his horse off the platform.

Que faire? How was it humanly possible for any horse to win the Derby race without putting in an appearance? And how was Milky Way to put in her appearance if she was not allowed access to any Epsom train? A less wilful and persevering individual than Mr Bhosh would have certainly succumbed under so much red-tapery, but it only served to arouse Bindabun's monkey.

"How far is the distance to Epsom?" he inquired.

"Fourteen miles," he was answered.

"And what o'clock the Derby race?"

"About one P.M."

"And it is now just the middle of the day!" exclaimed Bindabun. "Very well, since it seems Milky Way is not to ride in the railway, she shall cover the distance on shank's mare, for I will ride her to Epsom in propriâ personâ!"

So courageous a determination elicited loud cheers from the bystanders, who cordially advised him to put his best legs foremost as he mounted his mettlesome crack, and set off with broken-necked speed for Epsom.

I must request my indulgent readers to excuse this humble pen from depicting the horrors of that wild and desperate ride. Suffice it to say that the road was chocked full with every description of conveyance, and that Mr Bhosh was haunted by two terrible apprehensions, viz., that he might meet with some shocking upset, and that he should arrive the day after the fair.

As he urged on his headlong career, he was constantly inquiring of the occupants of the various vehicles if he was still in time for the Derby, and they invariably hallooed to him that if he desired to witness the spectacle he was to buck himself up.

Mr Bhosh bucked himself up to such good purpose that, long before the clock struck one, his eyes were gladdened by beholding the summit of Epsom grand stand on the distant hill-tops.

Leaning himself forward, he whispered in the shell-like ear of Milky Way: "Only one more effort, and we shall have preserved both our bacons!"

But, alas! he had the mortification to perceive that the legs of Milky Way were already becoming tremulous from incipient grogginess.

And now, beloved reader, let me respectfully beg you to imagine yourself on the Epsom Derby Course immediately prior to the grand event. What a marvellous human farrago! All classes hobnobbing together higgledy-piggledy; archbishops with acrobats; benchers with bumpkins; counts with candlestickmakers; dukes with druggists; and so on through the entire alphabet. Some spectators in carriages; others on terra firma; flags flying; bands blowing; innumerable refreshment tents rearing their heads proudly into the blue Empyrean; policemen gazing with smiling countenances on the happy multitudes when not engaged in running them in.

Now they are conducting the formality of weighing the horses, to see if they are qualified as competitors for the Derby Gold Cup, and each horse, as it steps out of the balancing scales and is declared eligible, commences to prance jubilantly upon the emerald green turf.

(N.B.-The writer of above realistic description has never been actually present at any Derby Race, but has done it all entirely from assiduous cramming of sporting fictions. This is surely deserving of recognition from a generous public!)

Now follows a period of dismay—for Milky Way, the favourite of high and low, is suddenly discovered to be still the dark horse! The only person who exhibits gratification is the Duchess Dickinson, who makes her entrance into the most fashionable betting ring and, accosting a leading welsher, cries in exulting accents: "I will bet a million to a monkey against Milky Way!"

Even the welsher himself is appalled by the enormity of such a stake and earnestly counsels the Duchess to substitute a more economical wager, but she scornfully rejects his well-meant advice, and with a trembling hand he inscribes the bet in his welching book.

No sooner has he done so than the saddling bell breaks forth into a joyous chime, and the crowd is convulsed by indescribable emotions. "Huzza! huzza!" they shout. "Welcome to the missing favourite, and three cheers for Milky Way!"

The Duchess had turned as pale as a witch, for, galloping along the course, she beholds Mr Bhosh, bereft of his tall hat and covered with perspiration and dust, on the very steed which she fondly hoped had been mislaid among the left luggage!

CHAPTER XIII

A SENSATIONAL DERBY STRUGGLE

Is it for sordid pelf that horses race? Or can it be the glory that they go for? Neither; they know the steed that shows best pace Will get his flogging all the sooner over!

The Duchess, seeing that her plot was foiled by the unexpected arrival of Mr Bhosh, made the frantic endeavour to hedge herself behind another bet of a million sterling to a monkey that Milky Way was to come off conqueror—but in vain, since none of the welshers would concede such very long odds.

So, wrapping her features in a veil of feminine duplicity, she advanced swimmingly to meet Mr Bhosh. "How lucky that you have arrived on the neck of time!" she said. "And you have ridden all the way from town? Tell me now, would not you and your dear horse like some refreshment after so tedious a journey?"

"Madam," said Mr Bhosh, bowing to his saddle-bow, while his optics remained fixed upon the Duchess with a withering glare. "We are not taking any—from your hands."

This crushing sarcasm totally abashed the Duchess, who perceived that he had penetrated her schemes and crept away in discomfiture.

After this incident Milky Way was subjected to the ordeal of trying her weight, which she passed with honours. For—very fortunately as it turned out—the twenty-four hours' starvation which she had endured as left luggage had reduced her to the prescribed number of maunds, which she would otherwise have infallibly exceeded, since Mr Bhosh, being as yet a tyro in training Derby cracks, had allowed her to acquire a superfluous obesity.

Thus once more the machinations of the Duchess had only benefited the very individual they were intended to injure!

But it remained necessary to hire a practical jockey, since Cadwallader Perkin was still lamenting in dust and ashes at home, so Mr Bhosh ran about from pillow to post endeavouring to borrow a rider for Milky Way.

Owing, probably, to the Duchess's artifices, he encountered nothing but refusals and pleas of previous engagement—until, at the end of the tether of his patience, he said: "Since my mare cannot compete in a riderless condition, I myself will assume command and steer her to victory!"

Upon which gallant speech the entire air became darkened by clouds of upthrown hats and shouts of "Bravo, Bindabun!"

But upon this the pertinacious Duchess lodged the objection that he was not in correct toggery, and that, even if he still retained his tall hat, it would be contrary to etiquette to ride the Derby in a frock coat.

"Where are his racing colours?" she demanded.

"Here!" cried Mr Bhosh, pulling forth the cream and sky-blue silken jacket and cap from his pockets, and, discarding his frock coat, he assumed the garbage of a jockey in the twinkle of a jiffy.

"I protest," then cried the undaunted Duchess, "against such cruelty to animals as racing an overblown mare so soon after she has galloped from London!"

"Your stricture is just, O humane and distinguished lady," responded the judge, who had conceived a violent attachment to Milky Way and her owner, "and I will willingly postpone the race for an hour or two until the horse has recovered her breeze."

"Quite unnecessary!" said Bindabun. "My mare is not such a weakling as you imagine, and will be as fit as a flea after she has imbibed one or two champagne bottles."

And his prediction was literally fulfilled, for the champagne soon rendered Milky Way playful as a kitten. Mr Bhosh ascended into his saddle; the other horses were drawn up in single rank; the starter brandished his flag—and the curtain rose on such a race as has, perhaps, never been equalled in the annals of the Derby.

The rival cracks were named as follows:—Topsy Turvey, Poojah, Brandy Pawnee, Tiffin Bell, Tripod, Cui Bono, British Jurisprudence and Roseate Smell. The betting was even on the field.

Poojah was a large tall horse with a nude tail, but excessively nimble; Tripod, on the contrary, was a small cob of sluggish habits and needing to be constantly pricked; Tiffin Bell was a piebald of goodly proportions; and Roseate Smell was of same sex as Milky Way, though more vixenish in character.

Not long after the start Mr Bhosh was chagrined to discover that he was all behindhand, and he almost despaired of overtaking any of his fore-runners. Moreover, he was already oppressed by painful soreness, due to so constantly coming in contact with the saddle during his ride from London—but "in for a penny, in for a pound of flesh," and he plodded on, and soon had the good luck to recapture some of his lost ground.

It was the old fabulous anecdote of the Hare and the Tortoise. First of all, Topsy Turvey was tripped up by a rabbit's hole; then Roseate Smell leaped the barrier and joined the spectators, while Tripod sprained his offside ankle. Gradually Mr Bhosh passed Brandy Pawnee, Cui Bono, and British Jurisprudence, until, on arriving at Tottenham Court Corner, only Tiffin Bell and Poojah remained in the running.

Tiffin Bell became so discouraged by the near approach of Milky Way that he dwindled his pace to a paltry trot, so Mr Bhosh was easily enabled to defeat him, after which by Cyclopean efforts he urged his mare until she and Poojah were cheek by jowl.

For some time it was the dingdong race between a hammer and tongs!

Still, as the quadrupeds ploughed their way on, Poojah churlishly refused to give place aux dames, and Milky Way began to drop to the rear. Seeing that she was utterly incompetent to accelerate her speed and therefore in imminent danger of being defeated, Chunder Bindabun had the happy inspiration to make an appeal to the best feelings of the rival jockey, whose name was Juggins.

"Juggins!" he wheezed in an agonised whisper, "I am a poor native Indian, totally unpractised in Derby riding. Show me some magnanimous action, and allow Milky Way to take first prize, Juggins!"

But Mr Juggins responded that he earnestly desired that Poojah should obtain said prize, and applied a rather severe whipsmack to his willing horse.

"My mare is the favourite, Juggins!" pleaded Mr Bhosh. "By defeating her you will land yourself in the bad odour of the oi polloi. Have you considered that, Juggins?"

Juggins's only reply was to administer more whip-smacks, but Chunder Bindabun persevered. "Consider my hard case, Juggins! If I am beaten, I lose both a placens uxor and the pot of money. If, on the other hand, I come in first at the head of the winning pole I promise to share my entire fortune with you!"

Upon this, the kind-hearted and venial equestrian relented, warmly protesting that he would rather be a proxime accessit and second fiddle than deprive another human being of all his earthly felicity, and accordingly he reined in his impetuous courser with such consummate skill that Milky Way forged ahead by the length of a nose.

Thus they galloped past the Grand Stand, and, as Mr Bhosh gazed upwards and descried the elegant form of the Princess Petunia standing upon the topmost roof, he was so exalted with jubilation that he elevated himself in his stirrups; and waving his cap in a chivalrous salute, cried out: "Hip-hip-hip! I am rampling hi!"

"Then," I hear the reader exclaim, "it is all over, and Milky Way is victorious."

Please, my honble friend, do not be so premature! I have not said that the race was over. There are still some yards to the judge's bench, and it is always on the racing cards that Poojah may prove the winner after all.

Such inquisitive curiosity shall be duly satisfied in the next chapter, which is also the last.

CHAPTER XIV

A GRAND FINISH

Happy Aurora is a happy Aurora! Hip, Hip, Hip, Hip, Hurrah! Hurrah!

Dr Ram Kinoo Dutt (of Chittagong).

On the summit of the Grand Stand might have been observed groups of spectators eagerly awaiting the finish. Conspicuous amongst them were Princess Petunia (most sumptuously attired) and her parent, Merchant-prince Jones; and close by Duke and Duchess Dickinson, following the classic contest through binocular glasses.

"Poojah will prove to be the winner!... No, it is Milky Way!... They are neck or nothing! It will be a deceased heat!" exclaimed the excited populaces.

And the beauteous Petunia was as if seated upon the spike of suspense, since Mr Bhosh's success was a sine quâ non to their union. Suddenly came the glad shout: "The Favourite takes the cake with a canter!" and Duchess Dickinson became pallid with anguish, for, rich as she was, she could ill afford to become the loser of a cool million.

The shout was strictly veracious, for Mr Bhosh was ruling the roast by half-a-head, and Poojah was correspondingly behind. "Macte virtute!" cried Princess Petunia, in the silvery tones of a highly-bred bell, while she violently agitated her sun-umbrella: "O my beloved Bindabun, do not fall behind at eleven o'clock!"

And, as though in answer to this appeal (which he did not overhear), she beheld her triumphant suitor saluting the empress of his soul with uplifted jockey-cap.

Alack! it was the fatal piece of politeness; since, to avoid falling off, he was compelled to moderate the speed of his racer while performing it, and Juggins, either repenting his good-nature, or unable any longer to restrain the impetuosity of Poojah, was carried first past the winning-pole, Mr Bhosh following on Milky Way as the bad second!

At this the Princess Petunia emitted a doleful scream; like Freedom, which, as some poet informs us, "squeaked when Kockiusko (a Japanese gentleman) fell," and suspended her animation for several minutes, while the Duchess "grinned a horrible ghastly smile," as described by Poet Milton in Paradise Lost, at Mr Bhosh's shocking defeat and her own gain of a million, though all true sportsmen present deeply sympathised with our hero that he should be thus wrecked in sight of port on account of an ordinary act of courtesy to a female!

But Mr Bhosh preserved his withers as unwrung as though he possessed the hide of a rhinoceros. "Honble Sir," said he, addressing the Judge, "I humbly beg permission to claim this Derby race and lodge an objection against my antagonist."

"On what grounds?" was the naturally astonished rejoinder.

"On the grounds," deliberately replied Chunder Bindabun, "that he surreptitiously did pull his horse's head."

Juggins was too dumbfoundered to reply to the accusation, and several spectators came forward to testify that they had personally witnessed him curbing his steed, and—it being contrary to the lex non scripta of turf etiquette to pull at a horse's head when he is winning—Juggins was very ignominiously plucked by the Jockey's Club.

The Duchess made the desperate attempt to argue that, if Juggins was a pot, Mr Bhosh was a kettle of equally dark complexion, since he also had reined up before attaining the goal—but Chunder Bindabun was able easily to show that he had done so, not with any intention to forfeit his stakes, but merely to salute his betrothed, whereas Juggins had pulled to prevent his horse from achieving the conquest.

So, to Mr Bhosh's inexpressible delight, the Derby Cup, full as an egg with golden sovereigns, was awarded to him, and the notorious blue ribbon was pinned by the judge upon his proud and heaving bosom.

But, as he was reverting, highly elated, to the side of his beloved amidst the acclamations of the multitude, the disreputable Juggins had the audacity to pluck his elbow and demand the promised quid pro quo.

"For what service?" inquired Chunder Bindabun in amazement.

"Why, did you not promise me the moiety of your fortune, honble Sir," was the reply, "if I allowed you to be the winner?"

Mr Bhosh was of an exceptionally mild, just disposition, but such a piece of cheeky chicanery as this aroused his fiercest indignation and rendered him cross as two sticks. "O contemptible trickster!" he said, in terrific tones, "my promise (as thou knowest well) was on condition that I was first past the winning-pole. Whereas—owing to thy perfidy—I was only the bad second. Do not attempt to hunt with the hare and run with hounds. Depart to lower regions!"

And Juggins slinked into obscurity with fallen chops.

Benevolent and forbearing readers, this unassuming tale is near its finis. Owing to his brilliant success at the Derby, Mr Bhosh was now rolling on cash, and, as the prediction of the Astrologer-Royal was fulfilled, there was no longer any objection to his union with the Princess Jones, with whom he accordingly contracted holy matrimony, and now lives in great splendour at Shepherd's Bush, since all his friends earnestly besought him that he was not to return to India. He therefore naturalised himself as a full-blooded British, and further adopted a coat-of-arms from the Family Herald, with a splendidly lofty crest, and the motto "Sans Peur et Sans Reproche." ("Not being funky myself, I do not reproach others with said failing"—free translation.)

But what of the wicked Duchess? I have to record that, being unable to pay the welsher her bet of a million pounds, she was solemnly pronounced a bankruptess and incarcerated (by a striking instance of the tit-for-tat of Fate) in the identical Old Bailey cell to which she had consigned Chunder Bindabun!

And in her case the gaoler's fair daughter, Miss Caroline, did not exhibit the same softheartedness. Mr Bhosh and his Princess-bride, being both of highly magnanimous idiosyncrasies, for some time visited their relentless foe in her captivity, carrying her fruit and flowers and sweets of inexpensive qualities, but were received in such a cold, standoffish style that they soon discontinued such thankless civilities.

As for Milky Way, she is still hale and flourishing, though she has never since displayed the phenomenal speed of her first (and probably her last) Derby race. She may often be seen in the vicinity of Shepherd's Bush, harnessed to a small basketchaise, in which are Mr and Mrs Bhosh and some of their blooming progenies.

Here, with the Public's kind permission, we will leave them, and although this trivial and unpretentious romance can claim no merit except its undeviating fidelity to nature, I still venture to think that, for sheer excitement and brilliancy of composition, &c, it will be found, by all candid judges, to compare rather favourably with more showy and meretricious fictions by overrated English novelists.

END OF A BAYARD FROM BENGAL.

N.B.—I cannot conscientiously recommend the Indulgent Reader to proceed any further—for reasons which, should he do so, will be obvious.
H. B. J.

THE PARABLES OF PILJOSH

FREELY RENDERED INTO ENGLISH FROM THE ORIGINAL STYPTIC WITH INTRODUCTION AND NOTES BY H. B. JABBERJEE, B.A.

INTRODUCTION

I shall begin by begging that it may not be supposed either that I am the Author or even the Translator of the appended fables!

The plain truth of the matter is that I am far indeed from standing agog with amazement at their literary or other excellences, and inclined rather to award them the faint damnation of a very mediocre eulogy.

But it so happens that the actual translator is the same young English friend who kindly furnished me with a few selected poetic extracts for my Society novel, and has earnestly entreated me (as the quid pro quo!) to compose an introduction and notes for his own effusion, alleging that it is a sine quâ non nowadays for all first class Classics to be issued with introduction, notes and appendix by some literary knob—otherwise they speedily become obsolete and still-born.

Therefore I readily consented to oblige him, although I am no au fait in the Styptic dialect, and cannot therefore be held answerable for the accuracy of my friend's translation, which he admits himself is of a rather free description.

Of the Philosopher who composed these Proverbs or Fables little is known, even in his own country, except that (as all Scholiasts are aware) he was born on the 1st of April 1450 (old style), and for some years filled the important and responsible post of Archi-mandrake of Paraprosdokian. He probably met with a violent end.

I shall not undertake to provide a note to every parable, but only in cases where I think that the Parabolist is not quite as luminous as the nose on one's face, and needs the services of an experienced interpreter.
H. B. J.

The Butterfly visited so many flowers that she fell sick of a surfeit of nectar. She called it "Nervous Breakdown."

"Instead of vainly lamenting over those we have lost," said the young Cuckoo severely, to the Father and Mother Sparrow, "it seems to me that you should be rejoicing that I am still spared to you!"

Note.—A mere plagiaristic adaptation of the trite adage concerning the comparative values of birds in the hand and in the bush.—H. B. J.

"I am old enough to be thy Grandfather!" the Egg informed the Chicken.

"In that case," replied the Chicken, "it is high time thou bestirredst thyself!"

"Not so!" said the Egg, "since the longer I remain quiescent, the fitter I shall be for the career that is destined for me."

"Indeed," inquired the Chicken, "and what may that be?"

"Politics!" answered the Egg with importance.

And the Chicken pondered long over that saying.

Note.—I must confess to following the Chicken's precedent, without arriving at any solution. For, logically, an Egg must be the junior of any Chicken. And again, even for parabolical purposes, it is far-fetched to represent an Egg as a potential Member of Parliament. On the whole, I am not entirely satisfied that my young friend is so proficient in acquaintance with Cryptic as he has represented to me.—H. B. J.

There is only one thing that irritateth a woman more than the man who doth not understand her, and that is the man who doth.

A certain Artificer constructed a mechanical Serpent which was so marvellously natural that it bit him in the back. "Had I but another hour to live," he lamented in his last agonies, "I would have patented the invention!"

The Woman was so determined to be independent of Man that she voluntarily became the slave of a Machine.

Note.—I do not understand the meaning of the Fabulist here.—H. B. J.

"She used to be so fresh; but she is gone off terribly since I first knew her!" said the Slug of the Strawberry.

Note.—See my remark on the last parable.—H. B. J.

"Now, I call that downright Plagiarism!" observed the Ass, when he heard the Lion roar.

"A cheery laugh goes a long way in this world!" remarked the Hyena.

"But a bright smile goes further still!" said the Alligator, as he took him in.

Note.—If the honble Philosopher is censuring here merely the assumption of hilarity and not ordinary quiet facetiousness, I am entirely with him. But I rather regard him as a total deficient in Humour and fanatically opposed to it in any form.—H. B. J.

"I trust I have now made myself perfectly clear?" observed the Cuttlefish, after discharging his ink.

The Cockney was assured that, if he placed the Sea-shell to his ear, he would hear the murmur of Ocean.

But all he caught distinctly was the melody of negro minstrels.

"It is some satisfaction to feel that we have both been sacrificed in a thoroughly deserving cause!" said the Brace-button, complacently, to the Threepenny Bit, as they met in the Offertory Bag.

Note.—This must be some local allusion, for I do not know what sort of receptacle an Offertory Bag may be, or why such articles should be inserted therein.—H. B. J.

Mistrust the Bridegroom who appeareth at his wedding with sticking-plaster on his chin [or "without sticking-plaster," &c.—the Styptic is capable of either interpretation.—Trans.].

Note.—Then I will humbly say that it must be a peculiarly elastic tongue. But in either form the Proverb is meaningless.—H. B. J.

"What!—My Original dead?" cried the Statue. "Then I have lost all chance of ever becoming celebrated!"

Note.—This is an obvious mistranslation, since a Statue is only erected when the Original is already celebrated.—H. B. J.

"What is your favourite Perfume?" they asked the Hog, and he answered them, "Pigwash."

"How vulgar!" exclaimed the Stoat. "Mine is Patchouli!"

But the Fox said that, in his opinion, the less scent one used the better.

Note.—This merely records the well-known physiological fact that some persons are born without the olfactory sense. Emperor Vespasian was accustomed to declare (erroneously) that "pecunia non olet."—H. B. J.

"I wonder they allow such a cruel contrivance as that 'Catch 'em alive, oh!' paper!" said the Spider tearfully, as she sat in her web.

Note.—From this we learn that there may be a soft spot in the most unpromising quarters. Even Alexander the Great, who spent the blood of his troops like pocket money, is recorded to have wept at a review on suddenly reflecting that all his soldiers would probably be deceased in a hundred years. It is barely possible that Piljosh may have been a spectator of this incident.—H. B. J.

A certain Pheasant was pluming herself upon having become a member of the Anti-Sporting League.

"Softly, friend!" said a wily old Cock, "for, should this League of thine succeed in its object, every man's hand would be against us both by day and night; whereas, at present, our lives are protected all night by vigilant keepers, and spared all day by our owner and his guests, who are incapable of shooting for nuts!"

Note.—This is a glaring non sequitur and fallacy. I myself have never shot for nuts—but it does not necessarily follow that any pheasant would remain intact after I discharged my rifle-barrel!—H. B. J.

"It is not what we look that signifieth," said the Scorpion virtuously, "it is what we are!"

Note.—True enough—but the moral would have been improved by attributing the saying to some insect of more innocuous character than a Scorpion. Perhaps this is so in the original Styptic, for, as I have said, I cannot repose implicit faith in my young friend's version.—H. B. J.

"I have composed the most pathetic poem in the world!" declared the Poet.

"How can'st thou be sure of that," he was asked.

"Because," he replied, "I recited it to the Crocodile, and she could not refrain from shedding tears!"

"It is gratifying to find oneself appreciated at last," said the Cabbage, when the Cigar Merchant labelled him as a Cabaña.

"Don't talk to me about Cactus," said the Ostrich contemptuously to the Camel. "Insipid stuff, I call it! No—for real flavour and delicacy, give me a pair of Sheffield scissors!"

"The accommodation might be more luxurious, it's true," remarked the philosophic Mouse, when he found himself in the Trap, "but, after all, it's not as if I was going to stay here long!"

"People tell me he can shine when he chooses," said the Extinguisher of the Candle. "All I know is, he's positively dull whenever he's with me!"

There was once a Musical Box which played but one tune, to which its owner was never weary of listening. But, after a time, he desired a novelty, and could not rest until he had exchanged the barrel for another. However, he sickened of the second tune sooner than of the first, and so he exchanged it for a third, which he liked not at all.

Accordingly he commanded that the Box should return to the first tune of all—and lo! this had become an abomination unto his ears, nor could he conceive how he had ever been able to endure it!

So the Musical Box was laid upon the shelf, and the Owner procured for himself a cheap mouth-organ which could play any air that was suggested to it, and thus became an established favourite.

Note.—This is apparently designed to illustrate the ficklety of the Musical Character.—H. B. J.

"Do come in!" snapped the severed Shark's Head to the Ship's Cat. "As you perceive, I am carrying on business as usual during the alterations."

The Bulbul had no sooner finished her song than the Bullfrog began to make profuse apologies for having left his music at home.

To a Butterscotch Machine the Penny and the Tin Disc are alike.

Note.—Surely not if an official is looking on!—H. B. J.

"My dears," said the Converted Cannibal reverently to his Wife and Family, as they sat down to their Baked Missionary, "do not let us omit to ask a blessing!"

There is but one Singer whom it is futile to encore—and that is a Dying Swan.

"I am doing a series of 'Notable Nests' for 'Sylvan Society,'" said the insinuating Serpent, on finding the Ringdove at home, "and I should so much like to include you." "You are very kind," said the Ringdove, in a flutter, "but I can assure you that there is no more in my poor little eggs than in any other bird's!" "That may be," replied the Serpent, "but I must live somehow!"

"No outsiders there—only just their own particular set!" said the Cocksparrow, when he came home after having been to tea with the Birds of Paradise.

The Elephant was dying of starvation, and a kind-hearted person presented him with an acidulated drop.

Note.—It is well-nigh incredible that any Philosopher should be so ignorant of Natural History as to imagine that any Elephant would accept an acid drop, even if it was on its last legs for want of nutrition.

The conclusion of this anecdote would seem to be either lost, or unfit for publication.—H. B. J.

There was once a famous Violinist who serenaded his Mistress every evening, performing the most divine melodies upon his instrument.

But all the while she was straining her ears to listen to a piano-organ round the corner which was playing "Good-bye, Dolly Gray!"

The Performing Lioness kisses her Trainer on the mouth—but only in public.

The Candle complained bitterly of the unpleasantness of seeing so many scorched moths in her vicinity.

"I have taken such a fancy to thee," said the Hawk genially to the Field-Mouse, "that I am going to put thee into a really good thing."

And he opened his beak.

There are persons who have no sense of the fitness of things.

Like the Grasshopper, who insisted on putting the Snail up for the Skipping Club.

The Cat scratched the Dog's nose out of sheer playfulness—but she had no time to explain.

"After all, it is pleasant to be at home again!" said the Eagle's feathers on the shaft that pierced him.

But the Eagle's reply is not recorded.

Note.—Poet Byron also mentions this incident.—H. B. J.

A certain Painter set himself to depict a lovely landscape. "See!" he cried, as he exhibited his canvas to a Passing Stranger, "doth not this my picture resemble the scene with exactitude?"

"Since thou desirest to know," was the reply, "thou seemest to me to have portrayed nothing but a manure heap!"

"And am I to blame," exclaimed the indignant Painter, "if a manure heap chanced to be immediately in front of me?"

Before a Man marrieth a Woman he delighteth to describe unto her all his doings—even the most unimportant.

But, after marriage, he considereth that such talk may savour too much of egotism.

Note.-This is very very shallow. I have never experienced any such compunctiousness with my own wives.—H. B. J.

"I shouldn't have minded so much," said the Bee, with some bitterness, just before breathing his last in the honey-pot, "only it happens to be my own make!"

"Is the White Rabbit beautiful?" someone inquired of the Albino Rat.

"She might be passable enough," replied the Rat, "but for one most distressing deformity. She has pink eyes!"

When the Ass was asked about his Cousin the Zebra, he said: "Do not speak about him—for he has disgraced us all. Never before has there been any eccentricity in our family!"

The full-blown Sausage professeth to have forgotten the days of his puppyhood.

"Will you allow me to pass?" said the courteous Garden Roller to the Snail.

Had anyone met the Red Herring in the sea and foretold that he would one day be pursued by Hounds across a difficult country, the Herring would have accounted him but a vain babbler.

Yet so it fell out!

Note.—I shrewdly suspect that my young friend has made the rather natural mistake of substituting the word "Red Herring" for "Flying Fish."

It is not absolutely incredible that one of the latter department should fly inland and be chased by Dogs—but even Piljosh should be aware that no Herring could pop off in such a way.—H. B. J.

An Officious Busybody, perceiving a Phoenix well alight, promptly extinguished her by means of a convenient watering-pot.

"Had you refrained from this uncalled for interference," said the justly irate Bird, "I should by this time be rising gloriously from my ashes—instead of presenting the ridiculous appearance of a partially roasted Fowl!"

Note.—I can offer no explanation of this allegory, except to remind the reader that the Phoenix is the notorious symbol for a fire insurance.—H. B. J.

"Alas!" sighed the Learned Pig, while expiring from inflammation of the brain, brought on by a laborious endeavour to ascertain the sum of two and two, "Why, why was I cursed with Intellect?"

"I shall know better another time!" gasped the Fish, as he lay in the Landing-net.

A certain Merchant sold a child a sharp sword. "Thou hast done wrong in this," remonstrated a Sage, "since the child will assuredly wound either himself or some other."

"I shall not be responsible," cried the Merchant, "for, in selling the sword, I did recommend the child to protect the point with a cork!"

A certain grain of Millet fell out of a sack in which it was being carried into the City, and was soon trampled in the dust.

"I am lost!" cried the Millet-seed. "Yet I do not repine so much for myself as for those countless multitudes who, deprived of me, are now doomed to perish miserably of starvation!"

"I have given up dancing," said the Tongs, "for they no longer dance with the Elegance and Grace that were universal in my young days!"

"But for the Mercy of Providence," said the Fox, piously, to the Goose whom he found in a trap that had been set for himself, "our respective situations might now be reversed!"

"She really sang quite nicely," remarked the Cuckoo, after she had been to hear the Nightingale one evening, "but it's a pity her range is so sadly limited!"

The Mendicant insisted on making his Will:

"But what hast thou to leave when thou diest?" cried the Scribe.

"As much as the richest," he replied; "for when I die, I leave the entire World!"

Note.—This is (if not incorrectly translated) a grotesque and puerile allegation. The veriest tyro is aware that when a Millionaire hops the twig of his existence, he leaves more behind him than a mere Mendicant!—H. B. J.

"Forgive me," said the Toad to the Swallow, "but, although you may not be aware of it, you are flying on totally false principles!"

"Am I?" said the Swallow meekly. "I'm so sorry! Do you mind showing me how you do it?"

"I don't fly myself," said the Toad, with an air of superiority. "I've other things to do—but I have thoroughly mastered the theory of the Art."

"Then teach me the theory!" said the Swallow.

"Willingly," said the Toad; "my fee—to you—will be two worms a lesson."

"I can't bear to think that no one will weep for me when I am gone!" said the sentimental Fly, as he flew into the eye of a Moneylender.

Note.—Cf. Poet Byron: "'Tis sweet to know there is an eye will mark Our coming, and look brighter when we come!"—H. B. J.

A certain Cockatrice, feeling sociably inclined, entered a Mother's Meeting, bent upon making himself agreeable—but was greatly mortified to find himself but coldly received.

"Women are so particular about trifles!" he reflected bitterly. "I know I said 'Good Afternoon' with my mouth full—but, as I explained, I had just been lunching at the Infant School!"

"I want to be useful!" said the Silkworm, as she sat down and "set" a sock for a Decayed Centipede.

A Traveller demanded hospitality from fourteen Kurds, who were occupying one small tent.

"Enter freely," said the Kurds, "but we must warn thee that thou wilt find the atmosphere exceedingly unpleasant—for, by some inadvertence, we have greased our boots from a jar of Attar of Roses!"

Note.—Once more I do not entirely fathom the Fabulist's meaning—unless it is that such a valuable cosmetic as Attar of Roses may become so deteriorated as to offend even the nostril organ of a Kurd.—H. B. J.

A certain Basilisk having attained great success in petrifying all who came under his personal observation, there was a Scheme set afoot to present him with some Token of popular esteem and regard.

"If we give him anything" said the Fox, who was consulted as to the form of the proposed Testimonial, "I would suggest that it should take the shape of a pair of Smoked Spectacles."

Note.—The Satire here, at least, is obvious enough. Smoked spectacles are a very inexpensive gift.—H. B. J.

"How truly the Poet sang that: 'we may rise on stepping-stones of our dead selves to higher things!'" remarked the Chicken's Merrythought, when it found itself apotheosised into a Penwiper.

Note.—A young lady, that shall be nameless, once presented me with a very similar penwipe, which represented a Church of England ecclesiastic in surplice and mortar-cap.—H. B. J.

"I shall not have perished in vain!" gasped an altruistic Cockroach, immediately before expiring from an overdose of Insect Powder, "for, after this fatality, the Owners of the House will doubtless be more careful how they leave such stuff about!"

Note.—British Cockroaches, however, resemble Emperor Mithridates in being totally impervious to beetle poison.—H. B. J.

The Sheep was so exceedingly tough and old, that the Wolf had thoughts of becoming a Vegetarian.

Note.—When we see some person attaining Centenarian longevity, we are foolishly inclined to fancy that, by adopting their diet, we also are to become Methusalems!—H. B. J.

A certain Ant that had lost its All owing to the sudden collapse of the Bank in which its savings were invested, applied to a Grasshopper for a small temporary advance.

"I am sorry, dear boy," chirpily replied the Grasshopper, "that, although I am playing to big business every evening, I have not put by a single grain. However, I will get up a matinée for your benefit."

This he did with such success that, next winter, the Ant was once more sufficiently prosperous to discharge his obligation by offering the Grasshopper a letter to the Charity Organisation Society!

Note.—The application of this is that a kind action is never really thrown away.—H. B. J.

"I never feel quite myself till I've had a good bath!" said the Bird whom an elderly Lady had purchased from a Street Boy as a Goldfinch.

And behold, when the Bird came out of its saucer of water, it was a Sparrow!

Note.—Like many Philosophers, Piljosh would seem to have had no great liking for ablutions. But water which could transform a Goldfinch into a Sparrow must previously have been enchanted by some Magician, so that our Parabolist's shaft misses fire in this instance (as indeed in many others!). Possibly, however, his Translator has once more proved a Traitor!—H. B. J.

"Pride not yourself upon your Lustre and Symmetry," said the Jet Ear-ring austerely to the Pearl, "for, after all, you owe your beauty to nothing but the morbid secretions of a Diseased Oyster!"

"I am sorry to spoil your moral," retorted the Pearl with much suavity, "but, like yourself, I happen to be Artificial."

Note.—Inhabitants of glassy mansions should not indulge in lapidation.—H. B. J.

"Come!" said the Peacock's Feather proudly to the Fly-flapper and the Tin Squeaker, as the final illumination flickered out and they lay in the gutter together, limp and exhausted with their exertions in tickling and generally exasperating inoffensive strangers. "They may say what they please—but at least we have shown them that the Spirit of Patriotism is not yet extinct!"

Note.—This must refer to some Cryptic customs prevalent in the Parabolist's time. But I do not clearly apprehend what connection either tickling, fly-flapping, or squeaking can have with Patriotism!—H. B. J.

LAST WORDS

Here conclude the Parables of Piljosh, together with the present volume. That the former can possibly obtain honble mention when compared with the apologues of Plato, Æsop, Corderius Nepos, or even Confucius, I cannot for a moment anticipate, and none can be more sensible than my humble self how very poor a figure they cut in proximity to the production of my own pen!

However, indulgent critics will please not saddle my unoffending head with the responsibility, the fact being that I was vehemently advised that, without some meretricious padding of this sort, my Romance would not be of sufficient robustness to produce a boom.

But should "A Bayard from Bengal" unfortunately fail to render the Thames combustible, I should rather attribute the cause to its having been unwisely diluted with such milk and watery material as the Parables of Piljosh.

So, leaving the decision to the impartial and unanimous verdict of popular approval, I subscribe myself,

The Reader's very obsequious and palpitating Servant,

HURRY BUNGSHO JABBERJEE, B.A., etcetera, etcetera, etcetera.